Wednesday, November 24, 1954

Breakfast is done and Carter Jones has kissed his husband, Nick Williams, and sent him off to a meeting when the doorbell rings.

Two men are standing on the threshold and asking some pushy questions about Nick and where they can find him.

Smelling a rat, Carter says he doesn't know where his husband is and sends the two men, one speaking perfect English with a slight accent and the other as shifty as all get out, on their way.

Knowing something big is up, he calls down to the office on Bush Street and ends up talking to Sam Halversen, an operative who works for them at Consolidated Security.

Within a few minutes, Sam has run up to the top of Nob Hill to fill Carter in on what turns out to be one of the strangest tales ever.

In the end, Carter has to ask himself: *How far and to what lengths will some men go for love?*

The Case of the

Jilted

First Secretary

Carter Jones Stories

The Case of the Jilted First Secretary

Nick Williams Mysteries

The Unexpected Heiress

The Amorous Attorney

The Sartorial Senator

The Laconic Lumberjack

The Perplexed Pumpkin

The Savage Son

The Mangled Mobster

The Iniquitous Investigator

The Voluptuous Vixen

The Timid Traitor

The Sodden Sailor

The Excluded Exile

The Paradoxical Parent

The Pitiful Player

The Childish Churl

The Rotten Rancher

A Happy Holiday

The Adroit Alien

The Leaping Lord

The Constant Caprese

The Shameless Sodomite

The Harried Husband

The Stymied Star

The Roving Refugee

The Perfidious Parolee

The Derelict Dad

The Shifting Scion

The Beloved Bach

The Redemptive Rifleman

The Agitated Actress

The Manic Mechanic

The Loveless Lawyer

The Crooked Colonel

The Crying Cowboy

The Rowdy Renegade

The Sordid Socialite

The Useful Uncle

The Seductive Sellout

The Case of the Jilted First Secretary

A Carter Jones Story

By Frank W. Butterfield

Published With Delight

By The Author

MMXXI

The Case of the Jilted First Secretary

Be the first to know about new releases:

frankwbutterfield.com

CJ01-D-20230105

Contents

Preface

From a hurricane-proof apartment
Daytona Beach, Fla.
Wednesday, April 14, 2021

Howdy!

If this is the first of my books that you're picking up, welcome! This story does stand alone even though it's nestled among and intertwined with other titles already published. The prologue will introduce you to the main characters and how they got to be where they are when this tale begins. Don't worry. As anyone who knows him will tell you, you're in good hands with Carter Jones at the helm.

If you're already familiar with my writing, allow me to introduce you to this, the first book in a new series that I'm calling the Carter Jones Stories.

Nick Williams and Carter Jones are the primary characters in the Nick Williams Mysteries series. That series of books starts in 1953, after the two men have been together for six years. Nick is the narrator of

1

those books.

This story, which is set around Thanksgiving of 1954, is told to us by Carter. This gives us new and delightful insights into how complex a man he happens to be and how what he sees differs from what Nick has been telling us about all this time.

You will likely find a few contradictions as you read along. And that's good! We all see things from our own unique perspectives. Nick and Carter are no different than anyone else in that respect.

In terms of the chronology of stories recounted in the Nick Williams Mysteries, this book occurs after *The Voluptuous Vixen* and before *The Timid Traitor*.

Enjoy!

Prologue: A new hire.

Offices of Consolidated Security, Inc.
777 Bush Street
San Francisco, Cal.
Tuesday, November 23, 1954
Just past 10 in the morning

Carter Jones a tall, muscled, and handsome former fireman was sitting at his desk in his office and sipping his coffee as he read through Saturday's edition of *The Californian*, the daily newspaper published down in Salinas. He was amused to see another story about poor Mrs. Vanderbilt, the fifth wife of Cornelius, Jr., who'd divorced her in Reno and hadn't paid any alimony or, if he had, it wasn't enough to keep his latest wife in style. She'd had to leave her New York City hotel digs and was applying for relief from the welfare board. Carter wasn't sure she was really as broke as she made herself out to be. Whatever the truth was, she was getting a lot of press.

He was reading through a stack of area newspapers

that a kid from a local newsstand brought by every morning. It was how he kept track of whenever a small town had a suspicious fire. Whenever he read a story like that, he'd drive over and offer his arson investigation services to the chief. He didn't always get hired, but he did more often than he would have thought possible just a year earlier when the idea first came to him.

He looked up when he heard a knock on his office door. Folding the paper, he said, "Come in."

Marnie LeBeau, their indefatigable office secretary, opened the door and stepped aside. Pointing to a kid in a brown suit, she said, "Carter Jones? Meet Brian Radcliff."

Carter stood and held out his hand. "Brian? Nice to meet you."

The kid stepped into the office, gave him a firm grip in return, and smiled nervously. "Thanks, Mr. Jones."

"Call me Carter. We all go by our first names around here."

Marnie nodded and said, "Mike's out for the morning but since Brian was a fireman, Nick thought you could fill him on how things work around here. Dawson and Andy will be taking him out for lunch at half past 11. I think they wanna drive out to the Cliff House so he can see the ocean."

Carter nodded. "Sounds good." He looked down at the kid. "You want any coffee?"

"No," replied Brian, rubbing his hands together nervously. "I'm fine. Thanks."

Marnie grinned at Carter and said, "I'll be at my desk if you need anything."

Carter said, "Thanks," as she closed the door. He then pointed to the chair next to his desk. "Have a seat and let's get to know one another."

Brian sat as Carter walked around his desk and did

the same thing.

Leaning back in his chair, Carter smiled. "I know a bit about your background and why you're here, but I'd like to hear your version of why you became a fireman and how you ended up here."

The kid nodded. "Sure." He took a deep breath. "I'm the third of five boys and grew up in Dayton, Ohio. I graduated high school in 1946. And, I guess you could say I wanted to be a fireman because of my uncle, Dale. He was a fireman who worked in Xenia."

"That's in Ohio, too, right?"

"Yes, sir."

Carter smiled. "How old are you, Brian? 26? 27?"

"Just turned 27 last month." Carter thought he looked young for his age. He would have guessed he was just out of college.

"I'm only 34, so I'm much too young for you to call me, 'sir'. Like I said, we're all on a first-name basis around here."

The kid nodded.

"When'd you start your training?"

"Right outta high school. In July of '46."

"I read that you were in Korea."

"Yes, sir." Brian frowned a little. "I was inducted in September of '49 and served through to June of '52. I trained at Fort Lewis in Washington State, near Tacoma, and then deployed to the 546th Engineer Firefighting Company in Kobe, Japan. By the time I got there, things were starting up in Korea. My unit was sent to Pusan to work with local firefighters and that's where I spent the rest of my time until I was honorably discharged."

"And you went back to Dayton after that?"

"Yeah. I even went back to Station 4, which was where I started."

Carter nodded. "Any interesting calls?"

"Well, I wasn't on duty at the time, but I was eating dinner with a friend and we heard the initial explosion." Brian relaxed a little. "A gas truck at the parking garage next door to the city jail exploded." He crossed his arms. "Actually, there were three explosions. After I heard the third one, I left the restaurant and walked over to the scene."

"Did you end up working?"

"From the rear. I pulled hose and checked the connections. That sort of thing. It was a three-alarm and, for us, that meant all off-duty were called in." He shrugged. "It was a big mess. We'd just started using Aerofoam about then and that helped."

Carter nodded. "We use that here. Although, to tell you the truth, we use our own mix that we get from a company down in L.A."

"Makes sense. I heard that Aerofoam is kinda expensive."

"I think that's why." Carter tilted his head to the right. "So... you started training out of high school. Then you were inducted into the Army. Then you're back in your old fire house in Dayton." He paused. "How'd you end up here?"

Brian sat back and sighed. "It's like this. That dinner I left to go to the fire?"

Carter nodded.

"Well, I was with my guy. His name's Mark Zeller." Brian unfolded his arms and looked down at the floor. "Mark and I met..." He smiled to himself. "Let's just say we met out and about."

Carter nodded. "Got it." He knew the kid meant they'd probably picked up each other on the street or in a park or something like that.

"That was in the summer of '48. That night when the fire happened, we were having our six-month

6

anniversary dinner at a Chinese place called The New Canton." He took a deep breath and continued, "Anyway, we were on again, off again, but mostly on all the way until I got home in '52." He shrugged again. "Then, I don't know what really happened, but suddenly he was dating this girl and they were gonna get married." He looked up at Carter. "You know what I mean, right?"

"Sure."

"So, all that's fine and, in fact, I'm thinking that Suzy and Mark make a swell couple, and so I'm not that upset, even though I really miss the guy, you know?"

"Yeah."

"So, about six weeks ago, Mark shows up at my apartment and he's brought a bottle of whiskey and he wants to talk. One thing leads to another and we're both back at it again like it's old times." He sighed. "The next thing I know is that I'm at work and my lieutenant pulls me into a room and says how there's been some talk that I might be queer."

"How'd he find out?"

"Suzy's mother, Mrs. Bellechase, knows the chief and she went to him and said I'd made the moves on Mark and she didn't think he should have people like me working for the fire department." He stretched out his arms. "And I guess the chief agreed because the lieutenant fired me on the spot. He didn't ask if it was true or anything like that. He just fired me."

"Did he mention Mrs. Bellechase?"

"Nope. He just said the chief told him a citizen complained about me."

"That's tough."

Brian nodded, still looking at the floor. "So, I go home after being canned and then I head to the gym, you know, to do some boxing. And Mark comes in after

he gets off work and tells me he heard what happened."
He looked up at Carter. "That's how I heard about you
and Mr. Williams."

"Nick."

Brian smiled a little. "Yeah. Nick." He took a deep
breath. "So, I sent a telegram here and heard back from
Robert Evans within a day." Brian suddenly wiped one
eye with his thumb. "Next thing I know, I got a place to
live here and enough money to take the train and as
much time as I need to take care of what I needed to
take of back home."

"Are your parents still alive?"

He nodded. "I told them I got a job working on arson
in California."

Carter leaned forward. "Just to be clear, Robert did
tell you we're not hiring arson investigators right now,
right?"

He nodded. "Oh, sure. I'm gonna get my P.I. license
and work for Mr. Robertson."

"You'll probably be working for either Andy
Anderson or Frankie Vasco. Andy used to work for the
F.B.I. and Frankie is a sergeant who retired from the
New York City police."

"Wow," said Brian. "F.B.I.? Really?"

Carter nodded. "Like Marnie said, you'll meet him
when he and Dawson take you to lunch. Dawson
Runson was a lieutenant for the Washington Metro
Police before he left. He and Andy had been a couple
since the summer of '53."

"Are there lots of couples who work here?"

"There's three. Nick and me, Andy and Dawson, and
Mike and Greg Holland. Greg worked for the S.F.P.D. He
was a lieutenant when he quit. Just like Mike was when
he was fired."

"Fired?"

Carter nodded. "Don't you know the story?"

Brian shook his head.

"Well, it's like this. Last year, in May, Nick was working a job for a client and I was recovering from an accident I'd had on the job. I worked at Station 3 on Post Street."

Brian nodded. "How long were you a fireman?"

"We're always firemen, son."

Brian grinned. "Yeah."

"I started in 1939 and was just shy of 14 years when I was fired."

"You were fired, too?"

"That's part of the story. Anyway, Nick needed to get some inside scoop from a cop by the name of Ben White. Nick and Mike were lovers before the war and Nick asked Mike to reach out to Ben. We found out that Ben was one of us and had a thing for firemen."

Brian chuckled "I don't know how it was at your station, but I can't imagine having a thing for other firemen."

"They never take enough showers, for one thing. And, when they do, they never get clean enough."

Nodding exuberantly, Brian said, "Exactly!"

Carter grinned. "So, I worked with a guy at Station 3 by the name of Carlo Martinelli and, to make a long story short, I asked him if he would like to meet Ben and he said he would. In exchange for me doing that, Nick promised me a porterhouse steak dinner at the Top of the Mark."

"Nice! I really wanna go there."

"Nick and I will take you there after Thanksgiving and, if you want, drive you around town and show you the sights."

Brian blinked in surprise. "Really?"

"Definitely." Carter looked at his watch. It was nearly

11. He needed to speed his story up since he had a few more things to talk about before Andy and Dawson showed up at 11:30. "Anyway," he said, "while were having dinner—the four of us: Nick, Ben, Carlo, and me —George Hearst was also there with a few folks. Now, Nick's family has a history with the Hearsts and—"

"Do you mean the same Hearsts as William Randolph Hearst? Like in *Citizen Kane*?"

"George is William Randolph Hearst's oldest son. And, if you ask Nick, he'll say that Charles Foster Kane is not really like the older Hearst."

Brian was shaking his head. "This is so... I dunno. I feel like I'm inside a movie."

With a laugh, Carter nodded. "I know *exactly* how you feel. I'm from a small town in Georgia and sometimes I can't believe what my life is like these days."

"Wow."

"Exactly." Carter sat back. "Anyway, the long and the short of it is that Nick walked over and told off George Hearst for some of the stories he'd been printing in the *Examiner* and, before we all knew it, *we* were in the papers. Of course, we didn't know *that* until the next morning. But, before midnight, Mike, Carlo, Ben, and I had been fired." Carter grinned. "All because we knew Nick."

"Gosh!"

Carter looked around his office. "And that's how we got here and where Consolidated Security came from. Nick was inspired to start a private investigation and security firm. And he handed it over to Mike to run for us."

"And you do all the arson work?"

"I do as much of it as there is to do, which isn't as much as I wish there was. Carlo was working with me and then he and Ben moved down to L.A. and now it's

10

just me."

"I never did an arson detail in Dayton."

Carter wanted to talk to Brian more about how arson investigation worked in that fire department, but he had a small list he wanted to get through before the guy left for lunch. "So, I've asked about your story and filled you in on ours and how we got here. Do you have any questions for me?"

Brian looked down at the floor for a moment before asking, "What's it like to work with all guys like us?"

"Well, we're mostly like that but we do have Marnie, who probably works harder than anyone around here. She's been Nick's secretary for 4 years, back when they were just in that one office where you met Nick and where she and Robert have their desks. We also have Frankie's wife who works for us. Her name is Maria. And we have a couple of lesbians, but they—and Maria—work over in our temporary office on Pine, which is one block over. Speaking of that, did Robert tell you that we'll be moving at the beginning of next year?"

"Yeah. He said we'll be moving into a skyscraper."

"Well, it's 20 stories and it's down at the bottom of Post Street at Market. Our offices will be in the top floors."

"Neat."

"It's almost done. You should go down there and have a look. Or Nick and I can take you there after Thanksgiving. And speaking of that, did Marnie or Robert tell you about Thanksgiving at our house on Thursday?"

Brian nodded. "Yeah. They both did and so did Nick."

"You're coming, right?"

With a smile, Brian said, "Oh, yes. And thank you for the invitation. I figured I'd be at a cafeteria somewhere."

Carter smiled back. "I'm glad to hear it. But back to

your question..."

Brian took a deep breath. "I guess what I'm asking is about this office." He tapped on Carter's desk. "*Here*, it looks like it's just guys."

"And Marnie."

He nodded a little impatiently.

"I guess I'm not doing a good job of answering your question, am I?" Carter ran his hand over his face as Brian watched him closely. "Well, we have all types here and some are friendlier than others. Everyone is professional, of course, and..." Carter thought for a moment. He was looking for the right way to frame the thought he was having. Leaning forward, he said, "I think the thing that I see that's different than, say, when I worked at the station is that most everyone here is relaxed. We all get along and seem to enjoy the work we do. And, for the most part, everyone is happy doing the work."

"Oh! That makes sense to me."

"No one's watching us, examining every step we take. And there's no imaginary girlfriends." He grinned a little. "And the pay is a lot better."

Brian looked around as if someone might overhear. "I didn't believe it when Robert told me how much I would be making. It's triple what they paid me in Dayton."

"Things are a little more expensive here than in other parts of the country."

"Not that I've noticed."

"Well, that's good," said Carter. He took a deep breath. "I know that I didn't really answer your question. But I think that, after you've been here for a while, you might be able to tell me what it's like better than I can."

. . .

12

Carter was just about done with the other things he wanted go over, including how to get around the City using the cable cars and the streetcars, how the streetcars were never called trolleys, and how San Francisco was never called Frisco or San Fran, when Andy knocked on the door and poked his head inside. "Y'all about done?" he asked with a big smile.

Carter stood. "I think so." He looked down at Brian. "Come see me anytime you want if you have any questions or need anything. We're glad you're here and that you're working for us."

Brian stood and offered his hand. As they shook, he said, "Thank you, Carter. I feel like I'm right at home."

"He has that effect on almost everyone," said Andy with a wink before leading Brian down the hall.

Carter sighed and felt that little lump in his throat that he often got whenever someone new showed up at their door. He was grateful that, thanks to Nick's unquestioning generosity, they could help these men and women get on their feet, do good work, and get paid well for it. He shuddered to think what might have happened to Brian if he hadn't known about Nick Williams and Consolidated Security in San Francisco.

With that thought, he wandered down the hall to Nick's office where he found Marnie typing while Robert was talking on the phone.

Nick looked up from the pile of mail on his desk with a smile.

Wiggling his finger, Carter tilted his head to the left.

In less than a minute, the two of them were back in Carter's office with the door closed and locked and Carter had his tongue down Nick's throat.

When they came up for breath, Nick whispered, "What was that for?"

Carter ran his hand over the back of Nick's head, down his back, and gently patted his ass. "For you being you and for your Uncle Paul leaving you all that money and for all the good you're doing for everyone here."

Nick's milk chocolate eyes searched Carter's face. "I couldn't do any of this without you. You're the reason it's happening." He pressed his cheek against Carter's shoulder. "I love you, Chief."

"And I love you, Boss."

They went back to making love to each other and continued until they heard Robert knock on the door and say, "Uh, Nick? Carter? Marnie and I are going to lunch. Can you cover the phones?"

Nick stopped what he was doing long enough to say, "Sure thing, kid," as Carter grinned, suddenly realizing there was one thing he did at work these days that he'd *never* done at the station. But he didn't think he should tell Brian about that. Not yet anyway.

Chapter 1: Mysterious visitors.

1198 Sacramento Street
San Francisco, Cal.
Wednesday, November 24, 1954
Breakfast

Carter jogged down the circular stairs and towards the great room. He was on his way to breakfast after a strenuous workout earlier that morning at Sugar Joe's, a gym South of the Slot where he did most of his physical training, including boxing.

When he came around the corner, he found Nick sitting at the head of their redwood dining table. He was already munching on triangles of buttered white toast and strips of chewy bacon.

"Hey!" protested Carter. "What goes on here?"

Nick looked up with a grin, showing off his milk chocolate brown eyes, and said, "I couldn't wait, fireman."

Right then, Mrs. Kopek, their housekeeper, stepped

out of the kitchen and looked up. "Mr. Carter, do you wish breakfast?"

Nodding, he replied, "Yes, ma'am."

"Coffee, yes?"

"Please."

She disappeared back into the kitchen as Carter slid into the chair on Nick's right. Helping himself to a slice of bacon from his husband's plate, Carter asked, "What's on your calendar for today, Boss?"

"Well," replied Nick as he wiped his mouth off with his napkin, "I'm meeting Henry at the building site."

"What's that about?"

"No idea." Nick looked at his watch. "I told him I'd be there at half past 8. I should get going. How's the fog out there?"

"Thick," replied Carter. "I had to take it slow on my way home from the gym."

"Did Ferdinand go with you?"

Carter nodded. "Yes. He's really coming along."

"Have you seen him smile yet?" asked Nick as he stood.

"Nora says he's just not that type."

Nick walked around and leaned over to plant a long and lingering kiss on Carter's lips. "I know what type I am," he whispered.

"What type is that?" asked Carter as he kissed back.

"I'm a grade-A, fully inspected, over-the-Moon lover of one Carter Woodrow Wilson Jones."

"That so?"

Nick stood up and nodded. "You bet it is."

"What about lunch?"

"Since tomorrow's gonna be a Thanksgiving feast for the ages, I was thinking about something simple."

"I was thinking the same. How about Mildred's?"

"Sounds good," replied Nick.

"Give Henry a big hug for me."
"I will."

. . .

Carter and Nick had first met, eyes locking across a crowded room, in 1947. They'd immediately fallen in love and, starting that very first night, had split their time together between Nick's apartment and Carter's apartment, one that he shared with Henry, his best friend from childhood in Albany, Georgia. Carter and Henry had become lovers after running away from their hometown in 1939 and ending up in San Francisco.

Finally, in 1949, Carter had convinced Nick to buy a house and they found one they immediately fell in love with on Hartford Street in Eureka Valley. It had three bedrooms, a nice kitchen, and a great backyard, along with the best neighbors ever—a lady couple, Pam and Diane, who lived with a pair of precious poodles, Mitzi and Trixie.

Unfortunately, a bumbling set of wannabe mobsters had set fire to their house during the previous summer. Much to their surprise, Nick's father, Dr. Williams, had invited them to stay at his house, the one Nick's grandfather had built on Nob Hill. Once the dust cleared, Dr. Williams announced that he and his bride, Lettie (the former Leticia Wilson and mother of Nick's secretary, Marnie), wanted to move into a smaller home which turned out to be an apartment nearby on California Street. Dr. Williams handed over the keys to 1198 Sacramento and that was where Carter and Nick were now living.

When they'd moved into the house, all the staff that had been there since the 1920s when Nick's mother had been around quit *en masse*. They didn't want to work

17

for two publicly avowed homosexuals.

It was too much house for Nick and Carter to manage on their own. Fortunately, Mrs. Kopek, their housekeeper from when they lived in Eureka Valley, had taken care of everything for them. She'd hired a friend of hers from the old country to be their cook. Mrs. Strakova, it turned out, had been a famous chef in Paris before the war and her amazing cooking made that abundantly clear.

Mrs. Kopek had also hired four kids. They were two couples in two different ways. Ferdinand and Gustav were in love and they were married to Ida and Nora, respectively, who were also in love. Ferdinand was their gardener and chauffeur (when they needed one). Gustav was what Nick liked to call their butler, but he was also a valet. Ida worked in the kitchen alongside Mrs. Strakova. And Nora was their housemaid who helped Mrs. Kopek keep the big mansion clean as a whistle and neat as a pin.

The whole group was originally from Czechoslovakia. Mrs. Kopek had been in San Francisco since the 1930s while the four kids had escaped the Iron Curtain in the last year or so.

Ferdinand was a marathon runner and had taken the silver in the 1952 Olympics in Helsinki. Since he'd come to work for them, he'd also taken up boxing and weightlifting and, most days, joined Carter down at Sugar Joe's.

The poor kids had a tragic past. After the Olympics, Ferdinand and Gustav had been confined to what they referred to as a "special" hospital by the Czechoslovakian authorities. Ferdinand and Ida had been forced to marry as had Gustav and Nora. The government psychiatrists were trying to cure them of their homosexuality. Since it wasn't a disease, the

18

doctors had failed. That didn't keep them from trying all sorts of things, including electro-shock therapy.

Mrs. Kopek and Mrs. Strakova were consummate professionals. The four kids had quickly become the same under Mrs. Kopek's sharp eye. They all did great work and had begun to feel like family. But Carter had always felt a shadow lurked behind them all, particularly the four kids.

. . .

As soon as Nick left, Carter stood and walked into the kitchen. That was normally were they took their meals because the big table in the dining room was just too big for the two of them.

He pushed the door open and stopped in his tracks. Every single surface was covered with something. If it wasn't the turkey that Ida was trussing on the kitchen table, it was the pile of potatoes Ferdinand was peeling while sitting on a stool in the corner.

"Yes?" asked Mrs. Kopek as she looked up from the stove where she was cooking his eggs.

"Oh!" said Carter. "I wanted to eat in here, but I see y'all are busy."

Gustav smiled at him from a sink of sudsy water and said, "We start while you at gymnasium."

"And finish end of day," muttered Ferdinand from the corner.

Mrs. Strakova suddenly emerged from the garage with a bushel of apples. She barked out something in Czech and then stopped when she saw Carter. "My apologies, Mr. Carter."

"None needed. I'll go back in the dining room and get out of everyone's hair."

"Hair?" asked Ida, looking up from her turkey. "What

19

hair?"

"It's an expression," said Carter with a big grin. "I meant that I don't want to bother you."

Ida nodded and went back to her ball of twine.

From the stove, Mrs. Kopek said, "I bring coffee and eggs in one minute."

Nodding, Carter said, "Thanks," and got the heck out of there before someone handed him an onion and a knife.

. . .

Carter had finished his eggs and bacon and was reading an article in that morning's *Chronicle* about how the stock market was finally back to 1929 levels when the doorbell rang. Realizing everyone else was busy, he jumped up, walked over to the big door, and opened it. "Can I help you?" he asked the two men in dark suits.

"We are looking for Nicholas Williams," said the shorter and darker of the two. His English was precise, but he had an accent that reminded Carter of how Gustav sounded when he talked.

"Nick's not here. Can I help you?"

The taller man, who was blond, held out a badge and then quickly pocketed it before Carter could get a good look at it. "My name is Reynolds. We need to speak to Mr. Williams on a matter of national security."

"Are you with the F.B.I.?" asked Carter.

"I'm with the government," said the man.

Carter knew something fishy was going on, but he wanted to find out what it was, so he stepped back and said, "Won't you come in?"

Neither man moved.

"Is Nicholas Williams here?" asked the dark man.

"No," replied Carter, getting more suspicious by the

moment.

"We need to talk to him," insisted the dark man.

"He's not here." Carter turned on his charm. "Are y'all sure you don't wanna come in? It's cold and foggy out here."

"No, thank you," replied the dark man.

The blond one said, "Do you know where we can find Mr. Williams?"

For a man from the government, that seemed like an odd question. Carter and Nick owned a private investigation firm called Consolidated Security, a fact that was easy enough to discover by consulting the phone book or a copy of Polk's. Considering it was past 8 on a weekday morning, the likelihood that Nick was at work was pretty high.

Carter smelled a rat and decided to shift gears. "Well, if you don't wanna talk to me, I'll let y'all go on your way." He shut the door without waiting for a reply.

He stepped back and watched through the window as they turned and headed up Sacramento to Taylor. He then ran into the office, picked up the phone, and called Consolidated Security.

. . .

"Hold on, Mr. Jones," said Robert Evans who worked with Marnie in Nick's office. "Let me see who else I can fine."

Carter sighed. He knew Nick was at the building site, so he'd tried to get in touch with Mike Robertson, the man who ran the company for them and had been Nick's first lover. He was also an ex-cop. But Mike wasn't around either. He wondered if maybe it would have been faster just to run down the hill instead of calling. But something told Carter he needed to take action right then. He had no idea why, though, apart from how strange those two men had acted.

After another moment, he heard Robert say, "I found Sam. Shall I connect you?"

"Yes, please. Thanks."

"My pleasure."

Sam Halverson was an older man in his 50s who'd worked for them for a few months. He was of Swedish extraction even though he was from the same part of Czechoslovakia as Mrs. Kopek. He'd been in San Francisco about the same amount of time as she. And, oddly enough, he was in love with her son, Ike, and shared an apartment with him in North Beach.

"Hi, Carter. It's Sam. What's going on?"

"I'm still at home and something strange just happened here. Two men showed up at the door. One of them flashed a badge at me and, when I asked if he was with the F.B.I., he just said he was with the government. The other one was foreign. In fact, his accent sounded a lot like Gustav's."

"Damn. I was afraid this was going to happen. Stay put and I'll be right there."

"Sam? What do you mean—" Carter stopped talking when he realized the line had gone dead.

. . .

The doorbell rang again not ten minutes later. Carter opened the door and Sam barreled his way inside. He was a little shorter than Nick, thickly muscled, and did not look as old as he was.

"Where's Anna?" He was referring to Mrs. Kopek.

Carter closed the door. "In the kitchen with everyone else. They're working on tomorrow's big shindig."

Sam grinned up at Carter. "Oh, yeah, I forgot we're coming over, aren't we?"

"Have you told her about you and Ike?"

"Not yet." He looked around and then pointed at the office. "Can we go in there?"

"Sure."

. . .

Once the door was closed, Sam walked over to Nick's chair and plopped down. "Look, Carter, we have a situation here."

Crossing his arms, Carter leaned against the door, and looked down at the other man. "What kind of situation?"

"The two men who were here?"

"Yes?"

"One was about my height, dark complexion, spoke very precise English?"

Carter nodded.

"The other was blond, about six feet even, and a little shifty?"

"Yes."

Sam took a deep breath and shook his head. "I don't know what these clowns want, but it isn't good."

"Who are they?"

"The first one works at the Czechoslovakian Consulate in New York, or that's what I hear, and I think the second one is a private dick here in town."

Carter frowned. "How do you know about the first one?"

With a shrug and a bit of a grin, Sam replied, "We Czechs, we all know each other."

"But you're Swedish."

Sam put his hands behind his head and nodded. "I am Swedish. Well, my father's parents were from Sweden. But my mother is Polish." He grinned. "Really, she was Silesian. And I was born in the Silesian part of the Austro-Hungarian Empire. But now I'm

Czechoslovakian, although I'm more Czech thank Slovak." He laughed. "Make sense?"

"And you told us you were from a place called Petervald, right?"

He nodded as he leaned back in the chair. "My father owned a store there. And that's where I met Anna."

"And when you and Anna—Mrs. Kopek—talk to each other, you speak in Polish, but when you talk to Gustav and the others, you're speaking in Czech? Right?"

Sam bounced up. "What is this? The third degree?" He started doing a boxer's step and pretended to swing at Carter. "I thought you were a fireman and not a copper." He took another swing.

In a flash, Carter grabbed his fist and held it.

Sam wiggled his eyebrows. "I always forget how strong you are."

Letting go of the man, Carter said, "What are y'all doing about this?"

"Y'all?" mimicked Sam in a perfect imitation of Carter's South Georgia accent. "Y'all ain't doin' squat." He walked over to the glass case Carter had set up for Nick to showcase all his "trophies" as Carter called them. "I just love this." He looked over at Carter and winked. "You two are the cutest couple." He leaned over and examined the contents. "There's your Super Connie, *The Laconic Lumberjack*, and that must be *The Flirtatious Captain*, your ship with its very handsome ship's captain. And a DC-7." He looked over at Carter again. "Have you found someone to make a model of the new office building?"

"No," replied Carter.

Sam stood and crossed his arms. "Why don't you like me?"

"I never said I didn't like you."

Nodding, Sam said, "True. But you don't trust me.

Why?"

"Let's get back to the matter at hand. Does Mike know about these two men?"

"Nope."

"Why not?"

"I was hoping to catch these two fish on my own line and reel them in without havin' to bother Nick about it."

Carter took a deep breath. "I know you have a crush on Nick."

Sam turned and looked down at the case again. "I do. And I'm smart enough to know better than to do anything about it." His voice changed. Carter thought he sounded more... Czech... and less American.

"So why not tell Mike?"

"You know how he is. He's a cop. And he plays by the book." Sam turned and looked at Carter. "I have a funny feeling about those two guys, and I can't quite put my finger on it."

Unable to help himself, Carter laughed.

"What's so funny?"

"So, did you teach yourself to speak perfect English by going to the movies?"

Sam grinned and nodded. "I sure did, pardner." He sounded like he was from Texas. "Why'd you ask?"

Carter was about to explain when he realized he shouldn't give all his cards away. He had a funny feeling about Sam. Carter knew the man was completely trustworthy when it came to looking after Nick's best interest, but he wasn't sure if Sam could be trusted as far as anyone else was concerned, including Carter himself.

"I just realized how much you talk like Humphrey Bogart as Sam Spade in *The Maltese Falcon*." That was true but what Carter didn't mention was that he'd realized Sam had a tell. Whenever he was telling something that was really, deeply true, he sounded more... Czech. Or maybe Polish. Whatever it was, it was different, and Carter decided to keep that little nugget of insight to himself.

Moving his mouth like Bogart did sometimes, Sam said, "Yeah? I betcha don't wanna make somethin' outta that, see?"

Carter laughed and shook his head. "No, I don't."

Sam sighed. "The truth is that I have no idea what those two are up to." He hooked his thumb over his shoulder and pointed towards the kitchen. "My best guess is that it has something to do with one or more of the folks who are cooking our Thanksgiving feast."

Carter nodded. "Why do you say that?"

"The Czech consulate?"

"Makes sense. And who is the blond guy? The one who claimed he was from 'the government'?"

"Oh, him I know from years ago. His name is David Bonnist."

"Bonnist? What kind of name is that?"

"Beats me. He has a private dick practice out in the middle of nowhere on Folsom and 18th Street."

"How do you know him?"

"From around." He shrugged. "You know."

Carter took a deep breath. "So, what can we do?"

"Do?" asked Sam.

"Yes. I want to make sure nothing happens to Nick."

A massive frown formed on Sam's forehead. "And what the fuck do you think I'm concerned about?"

Holding up his hands, Carter said, "I know, it's just that—"

He didn't finish his sentence because Sam had stormed past him and was out the front door in a flash.

Chapter 2: Making the rounds.

2190 Folsom Street
San Francisco, Cal.
Wednesday, November 24, 1954
Later that morning

Carter didn't have anything on his calendar for that Wednesday. Normally what he would have done was either hang around Nick's office and flirt with him or, maybe, drive across the Bay Bridge and do what he liked to call "making his rounds."

After Sam had run out, Carter had decided to go down to Bush Street and find Nick. But then, when he was parking his Mercury Monterey, he realized Nick's car, a Buick Roadmaster, wasn't anywhere up or down that block, which was where he normally parked it. Obviously, Nick was still at the bottom of Post Street meeting with Henry about the high-rise.

Carter decided to head across the bridge and go pay some visits to the fire chiefs in the small towns on that side of the bay. That was what he meant by "making his rounds." He would stop in at San Leandro or Alameda or Newark and chew the fat with whoever he found at the main fire stations there. He'd picked up a few arson cases that way in the last year and a half of building an arson investigation practice. He was in charge of that aspect of Consolidated Security's portfolio.

Technically, Carter worked for Mike who ran the company. However, Carter was half-owner and that meant Mike reported to him. Who reported to whom was insignificant since Mike and Carter tended to maintain a polite distance. As far as Carter was concerned, he liked Mike well enough. He certainly admired the man as both a former cop and a top-notch manager. But he did tend to think that Mike could be a little too much of a cop, just like Sam had said. Carter had often mused whether that was due to the difference between cops and firemen or whether that was due to the difference between the two of them. Either way, the détente they'd established in the last few months mostly seemed to work.

Not that there hadn't been some disagreements along the way, of course. But, for the most part, Carter let Mike do his job and vice-versa.

As Carter was cruising down Bush, he started thinking about what Sam had told him about David Bonnist. The man was obviously pretending to be a federal agent, something that Carter knew was illegal. The pay must have been good for him to take that kind of risk.

But who had hired him? Was it the man from the Czechoslovakian Consulate? And what were they up to?

Carter was running all that through his head when he realized he was about to cross Mason. Instead of going straight ahead, he made a sudden right. And without signaling, which wasn't a nice thing to do.

At Post, he made another right (sticking his hand out

the window to signal this time), heading towards Van Ness in order to avoid the mess that was Market Street. He wanted to find out about this David Bonnist person, so was headed down to "the middle of nowhere" as Sam put it. Of course, it wasn't nowhere—it was the Mission District.

. . .

On his way down, Carter had pulled over at the corner of South Van Ness and 16th Street to use a payphone. He'd called Information to get David Bonnist's exact address. Once he had that tidbit, he got back in his car, shifted over one block to Folsom and headed towards 18th Street.

Carter found a spot in front of a building whose sign announced it was the home of Ersek and Sons, cabinet and furniture makers. He'd circled the block of Folsom between 17th and 18th and had found David Bonnist's office. It was next door to the San Francisco Motorcycle Club, which looked more like a bar than anything else. There was a plastics company on the other side of Bonnist and then Ersek's.

Wishing he had a cigarette, Carter got out of his car and put on his hat. He walked around the front of the car and looked up and down Folsom, hoping he might find a newsstand, although that was unlikely in that part of town. Right then, a woman pushed open the glass door to Ersek's, stepped out on the sidewalk, and looked at him. She smiled and said, "Are you here for the cabinets? Are you Mr. Wickersham?"

He smiled back and tipped his hat. "No, ma'am." Looking right at the sign that announced they built custom cabinets, he asked, "Do y'all build cabinets?"

She nodded and then looked up and down the block.

"Yes, sir, we do."

Inspired by something he'd seen Nick do once, he said, "My name is Carter Jones and I'm in the market for some new kitchen cabinets. Could y'all build some for me, do ya think?"

She grinned, pulled the door open, and waved him inside. "Of course."

. . .

"This is Mr. Carter Jones," announced the woman to an older man sitting behind a desk. "He's asking about custom cabinets for a kitchen."

The man, who was wearing wire-frame glasses and had unruly black and gray hair, looked up and peered at Carter. "Yes?"

Carter took off his hat. "Yes, sir. I heard y'all can build cabinets for a turn-of-the-century house." Carter had never heard any such thing. "Is that true?" he quickly added.

The man, who was in his shirtsleeves, stood and removed his coat from a rack. He slowly pulled it on and, as he did, said, "We can build anything you want, Mr. Jones. Where is your home?"

"At Sacramento and Taylor."

The man stopped with one arm halfway in his coat. "Where do you say?"

"Sacramento and Taylor."

The man glanced at the woman. "My dear, Sheila, will you make us some tea?" He added, "With Mama's china, of course."

"Yes, Mr. Ersek." She quickly disappeared around a corner.

Carter could hear the sounds of people sawing and hammering. The air was thick with the smell of freshly cut wood as well as glue and the aroma of wood that was burning but wasn't actually on fire. As a fireman, Carter knew the difference.

The man finished pulling on his coat as he walked around his desk. "Young man, I wonder..." He led Carter back into the front lobby and then into a carpeted room with windows that looked out at the factory floor. Through the glass, he could see several men who were working with a couple of lathes, a band saw, and other equipment Carter didn't recognize. A round polished oak table sat in the middle of the room and featured a cut glass vase of red carnations in the center. "I wonder if you live at 1198 Sacramento." The older man was about 5'6" at the most and peered up at Carter.

"Yes, sir."

"That is the house that was built, not once, but twice, by Michael Williams, isn't that so?"

"Yes, sir."

An expression of mild distaste passed over the old man's face. That was quickly replaced by a look Carter had seen several times in the last few months. The man obviously knew Nick was Michael Williams's grandson and that Nick and Carter lived in that house together and slept in the same bed Michael Williams and his wife had once slept in. That was the first expression.

The second one had to do with the fact that Nick was one of the richest men in the City, quite possibly the richest. There was nothing like good old-fashioned greed triumphing over good old-fashioned bigotry.

"Are you thinking of replacing the kitchen cabinets, then?"

"Yes, sir."

The old man nodded. "I'll have to send my youngest son, Albie, out to measure."

"Of course." They didn't really need new cabinets

although he was pretty sure the ones they had dated back to the 20s. So, that meant they'd probably been replaced once since the house was rebuilt after the 1906 fire. He figured they were due for an update. In passing, he wondered how Mrs. Strakova would react, but then put that out of his mind to focus on what Mr. Ersek was saying.

"Now, if you wish to have a more traditional look, we have some very nice black walnut from Michigan that might go perfectly. We add a stain to seal the wood and it lightens up just a bit."

Sheila arrived right then with a tray. On it was a teapot, two china cups, sugar, lemon, a jug of cream, and a small plate of Lorna Doone cookies.

"Here is tea," said Mr. Ersek.

Carter smiled at Sheila as she set the tray down on the table. She asked, "How do you like yours?"

"Black."

She nodded as she poured out both cups. She handed one to Carter.

"Thank you."

She smiled and added one sugar cube to the other one along with a lemon slice. She handed the cup to the older man without stirring.

"Thank you, Sheila. Will you ask Edward to come in, please?"

"Yes, Mr. Ersek," replied the woman before leaving the room.

"If black walnut is too dark, for you, Mr. Jones," said the older man before taking a tentative sip of his tea, "we also have blonde walnut that might be very nice."

Carter nodded. He doubted Nick would like blonde wood in the kitchen but, then again, Nick rarely cooked anymore.

The older man put down his teacup and smiled.

"Here is my oldest, Edward."

A wiry man walked in and held out his hand. "Edward Ersek."

"Carter Jones." They shook.

"Mr. Jones lives at Sacramento and Jones," said his father.

"Grace Cathedral?" asked the younger man with a grin.

"No, Edward. In the Michael Williams mansion. The one re-built after the fire."

The son's friendly face turned to stone. "How can we help you, Mr. Jones?" His tone was as flinty as his face.

His father jumped in to answer. "Mr. Jones wants to replace the cabinets in the kitchen. I told him we could send Albie over to measure."

The son nodded. "Of course."

"And maybe some wood samples?" asked Carter, feeling as if he was wasting his time and their time and wondering if he'd been an idiot for just driving over without any sort of plan. He wanted to see David Bonnist, not buy new kitchen cabinets.

"Of course," replied the father. He picked up his cup of tea and had another sip. "I heard that you have a French chef who cooks for you. *La Zaza*? From Paris? Before the war?"

Carter nodded. "Yes. We didn't know who she was when she came to work for us."

"Yes," said the father. "I had a conversation with *Monsieur Verdier* about the wedding last summer." Paul Verdier was the president of the City of Paris department store near Union Square. He'd been at their house last summer when Marnie had gotten married to Alex LeBeau, whose parents worked for Mr. Verdier. Someone who was a friend of theirs recognized Mrs. Strakova as being the famous French

33

chef known as *La Zaza*.

"We're really lucky," said Carter. "Every meal we have is like going out to Ernie's or the Old Poodle Dog."

The father smiled as the son just stood there.

After an awkward moment, the older Mr. Ersek asked, "When would be convenient for my youngest son to visit?"

"How about next Monday at 10 in the morning? I think Mrs. Strakova is who he should talk to."

"Of course."

"And our butler, Gustav Bilek, will take care of all the details."

That seemed to impress the son who almost smiled again.

The father, however, was frowning. "Is that a Czech name?"

"Yes."

"How odd..." He sipped his tea and then put down the cup. "Very well, Mr. Jones, I will have Albie come by next Monday at 10 in the morning to take measurements and consult on the type of wood we should use."

Carter set down his cup. "Thank you, Mr. Ersek."

"Edward will see you out," said the older man without offering to shake.

He knows something about Czechoslovakia. Maybe this wasn't a waste of time.

Turning on his southern charm, Carter said, "It was a real pleasure to meet you, Mr. Ersek. Back in Georgia, my family is in the pine lumber business." He ran his hand over the tabletop. "It's always an honor to meet a craftsman who knows how to bring the best out of a piece of wood."

That seemed to please the older man. He bowed slightly. "Thank you, Mr. Jones."

"Pardon me, but may I ask you a quick question?"

"Of course."

"Have you met anyone else who was from Czechoslovakia lately?"

"Why, yes, as a matter of fact, I did. Why do you ask?"

Taking a shot in the dark, Carter said, "Well, I heard there was a man from the Czechoslovakian Consulate in New York visiting here. All the Czechs seems to know each other. Anyway, I wondered if that might be him."

"Yes."

"Now, I sometimes have a hard time with names. I seem to remember his first name was Ferdinand, maybe."

"Alexander, not Ferdinand," corrected the older man. "Alexander Sladek."

Carter snapped his fingers. "Of course! Alexander Sladek. Nice fellow, from what I hear."

The father glanced at the son and then said, "Well, goodbye, Mr. Jones. Thank you for your business."

. . .

Feeling a little bit proud of himself for having found out the name of the man from the Czechoslovakian Consulate, Carter decided to give the motorcycle club a try. Maybe he would luck into some tidbit about David Bonnist.

He strode confidently down Folsom, passing the plastics factory and its awful smell and then quickly walking by the glass front of Bonnist's office. He glanced inside and saw a blonde woman sitting at a desk looking bored as she flipped through a magazine.

When he got to the wooden door of the motorcycle club, he pulled on it and found it was locked. His watch said it was half past 10. There was no sign about the time they opened, but if it really was a bar, then the door wouldn't be unlocked until 11 at the earliest. Maybe they wouldn't open at all. It was the day before Thanksgiving, after all.

He thought about what to do next and realized the blonde was bored. That probably meant her boss was out. Of course, if Carter went in there with some story, he ran the risk that Bonnist might arrive back at any moment. With a sigh, Carter decided to risk it and headed back over to the glass front door and pulled it open.

The acrid smell of acetone hit his nose as soon as he did. The blonde had been painting her fingernails.

"Hello?" she asked as he walked down the short hallway and through the open door into the waiting area.

"Hi, there," said Carter, realizing he should have come up with a fake name before just barging in.

"May I help you?" asked the blonde as she looked up from her copy of *LOOK* magazine.

Carter took off his hat and held it against his chest. Using an accent he'd heard during his childhood in Georgia, he said, "Pardon me, but I was wonderin' if I might be in the right place to meet Mr. Bonnist? I have a problem I am so hopin' he can arrange for me." He also decided to bend over a little, something his history teacher used to do when he was asking questions about the War of Northern Aggression or something similar.

"Mr. Bonnist is out," was her disinterested reply.

"When do you think he might return? It's quite an urgent problem."

"Mr. Bonnist is on a very important assignment for a client." She looked at her pink fingernails. "May I take your name and phone number and have him call you?"

"Well, I just don't know. You see, I'm not from here

and I've yet to secure accommodations. Do you think you could recommend a moderately-priced hotel somewhere nearby?"

She snorted, still looking at her nails. "Not around here." She looked up at him and blinked. "You could try the Y.M.C.A. on Turk Street. They're kinda cheap."

Carter bowed a little. "Yes, ma'am. What a helpful idea. I really do appreciate it."

"You wanna leave your name and I can ask Mr. Bonnist to call you at the Y.M.C.A.?"

"That would be very kind of you. Yes."

She picked up a pencil and closed her magazine. "What's your name?"

"Howard."

She nodded.

"T. As in Toledo."

She nodded again.

"Albertson. A-L-B-E-R-T-S-O-N. Howard T. Albertson. I'm named for my mother's uncle who died in the Great War."

"I see." She put down her pencil and opened her magazine again. "I'll let Mr. Bonnist know you stopped by."

Remembering something Nick often did, Carter didn't move. He just watched her and waited.

After a few seconds, she looked up. "Yeah?"

"Well, I know I'm bein' more than a little intrusive, ma'am, but could you tell me if Mr. Bonnist ever does work with persons of a foreign persuasion?"

Her eyes narrowed a little. "Whaddaya mean?"

"Well, ma'am, my problem has to do with a man from behind the Iron Curtain. He lives in a strange little town I'm sure you've never heard of in Czechoslovakia." Carter overpronounced the name of the country. "It's a place called Petervald. Couldn't be more than a thousand people who live there, probably less after the war, doncha know, and, well, my friend..." Carter paused. "What I mean to say is that my *problem* has to do with a man who's from there and whose parents died durin' the war. They were from Sweden, you see, and..." He laughed nervously, like his late Aunt Maria used to. "Well, I'm sure this must be just as borin' as anything."

"Uh, huh."

"So, what I was wonderin' is if what I heard was true." He waited.

After a long moment, she sighed. "What's that?"

"Well, this fella I met on the Southern Pacific comin' up from Los Angeles, he's the one who told me about Mr. Bonnist and how he knew *all* sorts of people from Czechoslovakia and how he was just the person for me to see."

The woman rolled her eyes and sighed. "I really couldn't say."

"Well, ma'am, I can imagine Mr. Bonnist has lots of important clients and you can't just spill the beans on any of them to a total stranger."

She scratched her cheek with one of her pink nails.

"It would help me so much if you could just tell me if Mr. Bonnist has any connections to Czechoslovakia." Carter waited.

With another sigh, she said, "He might."

Carter fanned himself with his hat. "Oh, now, that really is a load off my mind. Yes, ma'am. Now I know I came to the right place. Howard T. Albertson. You have my name?"

"I do."

"Well, I feel so much better." Carter glanced out the window. "I guess I'll go find me a taxi somewhere and go back to the Southern Pacific station so I can get my bags and then I'll go check into the Y.M.C.A. You've really been more than kind." He grinned. "Would you mind if I asked your name?"

"Miss Owens."

"Well, Miss Owens, I just can't believe you're not a married lady, as pretty as you are."

She smiled just a little.

"Well, thank you, kindly, Miss Owens. I'll look forward to hearin' from Mr. Bonnist just as soon as he's available." He pointed his hat at her. "Now, don't forget to tell him. I'll be waitin' for his call, ya hear?"

. . .

Driving up Folsom on his way back to the office, Carter laughed at himself and the awful accent he'd used when talking to Miss Owens. It was a little after 11 and he didn't think Nick would be ready for lunch until noon or maybe a bit later.

Carter turned left on 6th Street and then headed towards Market. The sidewalks were showing signs of people heading out for an early lunch. At Market, he ended up sitting through an extra red light because a streetcar got stuck right in front of him. The driver had to get out and fiddle with the overhead wire. It sparked a couple of times, like almost always happened. Once that was done, the driver got back in and the streetcar was able to move on towards the Ferry Building. Meanwhile, the cars behind Carter were piling up and people were beginning to honk.

He finally made his way across Market and up Taylor. As he crossed O'Farrell, he looked over and had a sudden inspiration. He pulled into the garage in the middle of that next block, asked the kid to hold his car since he would only need 15 minutes at the most, and, thinking of Nick, gave him a five for his trouble.

. . .

"Yes?"

"Hello, my name is Howard T. Albertson, and I just arrived in from Los Angeles after coming all the way across the country from Atlanta and I don't have a reservation, but I was hopin' you might have a room for me. All I need is a single."

The man nodded as he looked down at something. "Yes, we can accommodate you. For how long will be staying with us at the Hotel Californian?"

"I reckon I might be here for as long as two weeks. I'm visitin' a sick friend who's in the hospital, you see, but I also thought I might stick around and take in the sights. I've never been to California, not to mention San Francisco."

The man smiled a little. "Welcome to San Francisco, Mr. Albertson." He pushed the book in Carter's direction. "Please sign in, if you would."

Carter wrote:

```
Howard T. Albertson
816 Peachtree Street
Atlanta 4 Ga.
```

He had no idea if such an address existed. But he did know that there was a Peachtree Street in Atlanta and 816 sounded like a good number.

"Beggin' your pardon, but may I ask how much the room is?"

"Of course..." The man looked behind Carter. "No luggage?"

"No, sir. I have it over at the Southern Pacific depot. You see, I wasn't sure where I might end up and didn't wanna drag my two valises around, if you know what I mean. I'll go and get it here in just a little while." He smiled. "After I freshen up and have myself a nice bit o' luncheon." He looked around the hotel lobby. "This sure is a nice place."

"Thank you, sir. The room is five dollars per night and that includes breakfast in our dining room."

"Well, that's just fine, sir. Just fine."

"One moment, please." The man walked over to the row of cubbies on the wall behind him and grabbed something before returning to the counter. He handed Carter a key.

"Room 808. Elevators are just to your left, past the phone booths."

"I thank you, kindly."

The man frowned a little and nodded.

. . .

Just in case the man was watching, Carter took the elevator up to the 8th floor. The room was a single, with one narrow bed and a small bathroom. Carter washed his hands to make it look like he'd been in the room and then left.

On the way down, a woman in a gray suit with a rose-colored hat got on at the 4th floor and looked up in surprise. "Carter Jones?" The woman was Mrs. Eloise Rafkin. She served on the foundation that Nick's stepmother, Lettie, ran. Carter had met Mrs. Rafkin a couple of times in the past few months while attending charity fundraisers. Her husband, a lawyer at a big firm on Battery Street, was on the boards of Bank of America, Transamerica Insurance, and the Union Oil Company.

Carter stooped over like he had at Bonnist's office

and said, "I'm afraid you have me confused with someone else, ma'am."

The woman blushed slightly. "Well, you may not know it, but you have a twin who lives here in San Francisco."

Carter gave her his goofiest grin. "Well, ma'am, they always did say my daddy was a bit of a tomcat. That might just explain it."

Her face went from blushing pink to red with anger.

The door opened right then, and the operator announced, "Lobby."

Mrs. Rafkin stormed out of the car and headed across the lobby.

Carter just smiled to himself as he sauntered over to an empty phone booth. He pulled out the phone book and looked up the number for David Bonnist's office. Once he found it, he picked up the receiver, dropped a dime in the slot, and dialed Mission 8-4545.

After three rings, he heard Miss Owens answer, "Private investigator."

"Miss Owens?"

"Yeah?"

"This is Howard T. Albertson. We spoke earlier this mornin'."

"I'm sorry, Mr. Albertson, but Mr. Bonnist isn't back in the office."

"Oh, that's just fine, honey. I just wanted to let you know I ran across that fella I met on the train and we decided to go in together for a hotel room instead of the Y.M.C.A. and I wanted to give you my telephone number here, if you don't mind."

"Yeah?"

"Yes, ma'am. I'm stayin' at the Hotel Californian. I think it's on Taylor Street, but I could be wrong."

"Taylor and O'Farrell."

Carter laughed. "Well, I guess you would know that since you're probably a native."

"I am."

"May I give you the telephone number here, Miss Owens?"

"Sure."

Carter read from the card that was mounted in a black frame on the wall above the phone. "It's Tuxedo 5-2500. Have Mr. Bonnist ask for me, Howard T. Albertson. I'm in Room 808, honey."

"I'll let him know. Goodbye." The line went dead before Carter could say anything else.

Chapter 3: Tomato soup and grilled cheese.

Mildred's Diner
Corner of Ellis and Van Ness
San Francisco, Cal.
Wednesday, November 24, 1954
Just past 1 in the afternoon

"Well, lookie here!" exclaimed Mildred as Nick led Carter into the restaurant.

Several diners turned to gawk.

Carter smiled at the Texas woman whose hair that day was Lucy orange. "Howdy, Mildred."

She grinned up at him and said, "Be right with y'all," before walking over to talk to a couple sitting in a booth.

Nick led the way to their usual table all the way in the back. Once they were seated, he said, "All I want is tomato soup and grilled cheese."

Nodding, Carter said, "That sounds good, although I

45

think I'm gonna ask Mildred to have Joe add a couple of slices of ham on mine." Joe was the cook who worked for Mildred back in the kitchen.

Nick smiled over at him. "What'd you do this morning, Chief?"

Before Carter could answer, Mildred walked up with a pot of coffee in her hands. As they both turned over their cups, she asked, "What's your pleasure for today?"

They both gave their orders.

Mildred nodded just as a plate crashed in the kitchen. She sighed. "That new fella I just hired to wash dishes is all thumbs." More darkly, she added, "This might be his last day."

Once she'd walked away, Carter asked, "What did Henry have to say?" He was hoping Nick would forget what he'd asked earlier. Carter didn't want to lie outright to the man he loved but he didn't want to tell him anything either. Not until there was something to tell.

"He took me up to the top floor. He wanted to know if we wanted it built out or not."

"What'd you say?" asked Carter as he sipped from his coffee cup.

"I told him to wait until we knew if we'd have a restaurant up there or not."

"Is that going to be a problem?"

Nick shrugged. "Henry didn't seem to think so."

"How's the building looking?"

"It looks like it's done, at least from the outside. The inside is still a work in progress, of course."

"Did you see your office?"

Nick nodded.

With a grin, Carter asked, "And how's the view?" He knew the answer already since he'd given Henry strict instructions to put Nick's office in the southeast corner of the nineteenth floor. The top floor—where a restaurant might or might not end up—was the twentieth.

"It's nice." Nick put a couple of sugar cubes in his coffee and stirred.

Carter tried not to frown in disappointment. He was hoping Nick would be excited about being able to see the Ferry Building at the end of Market Street from his desk. Carter didn't care much about views and such, but he knew his husband did. He'd watched Nick stare out plane windows for hours. He also knew that Nick loved to sit at the top of Twin Peaks in the middle of the City, particularly at night, and gaze out over all the streets and across the bay. Nick liked a good view.

"Henry and Robert are fighting."

"Really?" asked Carter. "What about this time?"

Nick shrugged. "You know how much I like Henry..."

"I do." Carter also knew that, when Henry was in a snit, Nick was a better friend to him than Carter could ever be. He and Henry had known each other since before either could remember since their families both went to First Baptist in Albany. Henry had been Carter's best friend and the two had gone through thick and thin. They'd also been lovers from the time they got to California to when Henry became an officer in the Army during the war.

After Henry came home to San Francisco, they went back to being friends and roommates. Henry was smart. He was a great engineer and a budding architect.

He was also a slob—never making the bed, rarely doing the dishes, hardly ever bothering to sweep or mop or dust—the list went on and on.

And he was prone to being a snob. When he'd been at

school at Cal in Berkeley, he'd always found plenty of rich kids to pal around with and, after the war and before he met Robert, only ever dated guys who drove fancy cars or had trust funds or the like.

And he still considered Carter to be his best friend and was in the habit of complaining to Carter about any and every single solitary thing there was to complain about. It irritated Carter and the truth was that he was just about at the end of his rope with Henry.

And so, it really got his attention to hear that Nick knew Henry was fighting with Robert (again) and Carter didn't.

With a frown, he asked, "What are they fighting about?"

Nick looked down at his coffee cup. "He says that Robert won't tell him about his family."

"So?"

With a shrug, Nick said, "My thoughts exactly."

Mildred arrived right then and laid out their plates. "Lookin' good?"

Nick nodded. "Great."

Carter grinned up at her. "Definitely. Thanks."

She winked and said, "Be back in a jiff with more coffee."

Once she was gone, Carter picked up his spoon and stirred his soup as he asked, "So why does this matter?"

"Henry says that, if Robert really loved him, he would come clean about his past."

"That's silly." That was a word Carter often used in his own head to describe Henry's litany of complaints.

Mildred was back and pouring coffee. She asked, "Soup too hot?"

Nick looked up at her. "It's fine."

She winked at him and then left.

"Did he ask you to do something about this?" asked

Carter as he took a bite of his sandwich.

"Yeah. He wants me to hire an outside firm to do a background check."

Carter looked up. "You're not going to, are you?"

Nick grinned. "I told Henry no outside firm in the City would work for us."

"How'd he take that?"

"With a lotta grumbling."

"How long did Henry go on and on about all this?"

"Not long," replied Nick, examining the triangle of grilled cheese he'd picked up as he ignored Carter.

"Son..." whispered Carter, "tell me the truth."

With a big sigh, Nick put down his food and looked at Carter. "The better part of 90 minutes."

Chuckling, Carter said, "Better you than me."

"That's what I don't get."

Blowing on a spoonful of soup, Carter asked, "What?"

"He told me he didn't want you to know."

"So, why are you telling me?"

"Because we don't keep secrets from each other."

With that kick to the stomach, Carter nodded, tried the soup, and grimaced when it burned his tongue. That immediately reminded him of one particularly colorful and long-winded sermon preached by Brother Wilkins at First Baptist. It had to be after the Depression had really hit hard in Albany, because he could remember that the sermon preceded a special collection for the local food pantry. In any event, one of the things Brother Wilkins had said and that Carter never forgot was how, in hell, the soup always smelled so good, but it was always too hot to eat. And being that it was hell, you could never cool it off, no matter how much you blew on your spoon.

. . .

Later that night, Carter was down to his underwear shorts and stoking the fire in their bedroom when Nick asked, "I keep meaning to ask you, Chief. What'd you do all day?"

Keeping his eyes focused on the stack of kindling he was building, Carter said, "This and that."

"Where were you this morning? Marnie said Carlo called from L.A. and was looking for you."

"This morning..." Carter paused.

"Yeah."

Deciding that telling half the truth was better than the whole truth, Carter said, "I was looking for new kitchen cabinets."

"New kitchen cabinets?"

"That's right. I went down to Folsom and 18th and talked to Mr. Ersek about new cabinets."

"Who?"

"Ersek. They're Turks. Top notch work. Uncle Leroy would have been impressed." Carter's uncle had once owned the lumber and paper mill that he now owned.

"Why new cabinets? Aren't the ones we have good enough?"

Carter poked the fire a little. "They date back to the 20s. Time for an upgrade." Wincing to himself, he added, "Don't you think Mrs. Strakova deserves the best?"

"Sure."

"We could give them to her as a Christmas present."

Nick laughed. "Look, Chief, I may not know a lot about Christmas presents, but I can guarantee you giving Mrs. Strakova a new set of cabinets as a *present* is a terrible idea."

50

Carter nodded since Nick was right.

"You coming to bed?"

With a sigh, Carter stood and put away the poker. He turned and saw that Nick was looking at him from the bed with a smirk on his face. "What are you up to, Chief?"

"Nothing," replied Carter as he slowly walked over to the bed.

"It's not nothing. You're definitely up to something."

Standing at the bedpost, Carter decided it was time to shut Nick up, so he began to slowly grin.

"What?"

Pushing his underwear shorts down to the floor, Carter stepped over a bit so he was in full view. He crossed his arms and flexed his biceps.

As Nick began to breathe hard, he said, "Carter Woodrow Wilson Jones, what are you doin'?"

Not saying a word, Carter just stared into Nick's milk chocolate eyes and gave him the final blow. He forced his mouth into a crooked smile.

Nick, being Nick, did what he always did and fell back on the bed.

"You ready for me, now, son?"

"Yeah," croaked Nick as he kicked off his underwear shorts and pushed back the covers. He turned on his stomach and scooted over so Carter had easy access and, in a flash, they were going at it like the big pistons in a ship's engine, something Carter had seen last summer when they went to Hawaii. He liked to imagine he was one of those huge pieces of metal, going in and going out. It was an image that always got his gears going. Always.

Chapter 4: A Thanksgiving party.

1198 Sacramento Street
San Francisco, Cal.
Thursday, November 25, 1954
After lunch

Nick smiled at Brian Radcliff, the new guy from Ohio, and asked, "How do you like San Francisco?"

"It's like nothing I've ever seen before. I think I'm in love."

Nick and Carter both laughed at that. Nick said, "I've lived here all my life and I agree. I haven't been to that many places, but I like the City."

"Well," said Brian, blushing a little, "your roots go all the way back to the beginning, right?" He looked up at Carter and then back at Nick. "I read this house came from Gold Rush money."

Nick nodded, his smile fading a little as always happened when the subject came up. "Sure. My grandfather built this place. But it was his father who came over from Wales and all that." Nick looked around and then nodded. "Excuse me. I need to go talk to my stepmother." His smile was back. "Glad you came over for dinner, Brian. Carter and I will take you up to the Top of the Mark next week, if you want."

"That'd be swell, Mr. Williams."

He said, "It's Nick, kid," as he walked over to where Lettie was standing by the fireplace and waiting for him.

Brian was about to say something when Sam walked up with a big grin on his face. "Swell place, ain't it?"

"Yes, sir. And everyone's so friendly."

Sam glanced at Carter for a moment before putting his hand on Brian's shoulder, squeezing it, and saying, "That's one of the great things about working for Consolidated Security. We're all so friendly."

"Will y'all excuse me?" asked Carter as he saw Nick's father walking out into the back garden. "I need to find Dr. Williams. There's something he said he wanted to tell me earlier."

Brian nodded. "Oh, sure, Carter. Thanks for inviting me. It's been swell."

Carter smiled, said, "Glad you made it, Brian," and strode over to the garden door.

. . .

"I am stuffed," said Alex LeBeau as he patted his stomach and grinned at Carter. The sky had cleared up after the thick fog the day before. It was nice for that time of year. Around 65, maybe a little warmer, and no wind to speak of.

Carter, Alex, Dr. Williams, and Mr. LeBeau, Alex's father, were all sipping from small glasses filled with Cointreau, an orange liqueur. It was something Mr. LeBeau had asked Ferdinand to bring out on a silver tray. While Mr. LeBeau poured, Ferdinand stood at attention, holding the tray perfectly still and with his usual stoic facial expression. Once everyone was served, he took the tray and the bottle back into the house.

"That is why, *mon fils*, I bring the *Cointreau* for after the large meal, *non*?"

Alex smiled at his father. "*Bien sûr, Papa.*"

The older man took a sip from his glass and smiled in return.

"Leticia told me about something odd that happened yesterday," commented Dr. William. He was looking up at Carter with a slight frown on his face.

"What was that?"

"Two men, one with an accent, stopped by the apartment yesterday morning and asked where Nicholas was. She didn't like the look of either man, so she sent them on their way." Dr. Williams grinned a little.

"I wouldn't wanna be sent on my way by Mrs. Williams," said Alex.

Mr. LeBeau said, "The same happened at the store."

"Oh?" asked Carter.

"*Oui.* Two men, one who was European, likely Polish, I think, came to see me in the afternoon asking about *Nicholas*." He tilted his head. "Is there trouble, do you think?"

Carter shook his head, hoping to turn the conversation if he could. "I doubt it. It was probably someone from the Internal Revenue Bureau."

"Or maybe the F.B.I.?" asked Alex.

Before Carter could reply, Dr. Williams pointedly asked, "Why would revenue agents ask about Nicholas at the City of Paris? That simply makes no sense, Carter."

"I have no idea." That was a true statement.

"I do not understand why all this from the government," said Mr. LeBeau. He shrugged. "I read *Nicholas* pays much in taxes. What else is there?"

"Sometimes," said Carter, trying to disguise his growing discomfort, "they think the folks at Bank of America aren't filling out the forms the right way." That was true. Or, at least, it had been in 1951 when Nick had been audited by the government for his 1949 taxes.

Dr. Williams stared at him for a hair longer than Carter liked and then turned to Alex. "How is married life treating you, young man?"

As Alex replied about how Marnie didn't like the fact that Alex was clumsy when it came to drying dishes. His father asked if he was really clumsy or if he was just pretending to be clumsy so he could get out of kitchen cleanup. As everyone laughed, Carter excused himself and headed back into the house.

. . .

In the office, Carter found Sam talking with Walter Marcello, their short, slight, owl-like resident brainiac who'd once worked as a cop in Albany (the town across the bay, not the one in Georgia). The two men were standing next to the trophy case.

Walter was smiling a little and nodding as Sam was saying, "And then I moved in on him and—" He stopped talking when he noticed his enraptured audience had stopped paying attention.

"Hello, Mr. Jones," squeaked Walter.

"Hello, Walter," replied Carter as he walked over to the two men. "Don't let me interrupt."

"I was just telling Walter about this soldier who was supposed to be guarding a meeting between Stalin, Bukharin, and Zinoviev, but who was really letting me fuck him."

Carter never knew whether to believe Sam and his wild stories about his sexual escapades in Moscow in the 20s or not.

"How's the party out there?" asked Sam.

"Fine," replied Carter. "I was looking for you at the office yesterday afternoon."

Sam shrugged. "Walter and I were out looking for our Czech friend."

"His name is Alexander Sladek," said Carter.

Walter looked up in surprise.

"Are you sure?" asked Sam.

"Yes, I'm sure. I talked to Mr. Ersek, the Turkish cabinet maker who's two doors down from Bonnist's office. He's the one who told me."

Walter's mouth dropped open as Sam quickly walked around Carter and shut the office door. "Does this thing lock?" he asked.

"No," replied Carter, turning around to keep an eye on the older man.

Leaning against the door, Sam looked Carter up and down. "Do you even have a P.I. license? You know it's illegal to investigate without a license in California, right?"

Carter rolled his eyes. "I've had a license since July of '53. And, yes, I know it's illegal because of all that bullshit that happened to Nick."

"Uh, Mr. Jones?" asked Walter in a quiet voice.

Carter walked over to the leather chair that was in front of his desk and sat down. From experience, he knew how much easier it was to talk to Walter when he was seated. The brainiac seemed to be intimidated by him otherwise. "Yes?"

"Well, uh, I guess I was wondering what all you did yesterday."

"Me too," added Sam, who was still leaning against

the door.

Carter sighed. "I was going to go over to the East Bay, but I decided to see what I could find out about Bonnist."

"You did what?" asked Sam.

"I went down to Folsom and 18th to see what Bonnist might be up to."

Walter glanced at Sam again.

"What?" asked Carter.

"You may have a license," said Sam, "but you're not a trained P.I."

Carter took a deep breath and reminded himself that these were his employees and, even if they couldn't respect him, he certainly owed them his respect. Sam, after all, had really come through for him and Nick in the year since they'd first met him. And Walter had helped get him and Nick out of jail up in Sausalito the previous summer. "I know I'm not trained." A wave of anger passed over him.

How dare they question me like this?

Then he reminded himself about respect. With that thought, he suddenly flashed on how his father used to treat his employees back in Georgia and took another deep breath. Whatever that asshole had done, Carter knew he should do the opposite. In as calm a voice as he could muster, he asked, "Do you wanna hear what I found out?"

Walter nodded as Sam said, "Definitely."

"When I got down there, I parked in front of Ersek's and then looked around. Their secretary came out and asked if I was there to pick up an order. It occurred to me I could talk to them if I went in and placed an order myself, so I did."

Sam snorted. "Whadja buy?"

"New kitchen cabinets," replied Carter, keeping his

father and his evil ways at the top of his mind.

Do the opposite! Do the opposite!

"Neat," said Walter as he peered at Carter through his round glasses.

"As I was talking to Mr. Ersek—the father, that is—I discovered that he'd met Bonnist's Czechoslovakian friend. He told me his name."

Sam looked mildly impressed. "Anything else?"

"I tried to go inside the motorcycle club, but they weren't open."

"That's a rough place. They don't like fags."

Carter nodded. "No surprise."

"What else did you do, Mr. Jones?" asked Walter. He seemed eager to hear more.

"I decided to storm the citadel and went into Bonnist's office."

"What?" asked both Sam and Walter in unison.

Carter shrugged. "I pretended I was in from out of town and that I met a man on the train who'd recommended Bonnist. I said I was having trouble with someone from Czechoslovakia and the secretary more or less said Bonnist did business with someone from there."

Sam crossed his arms. "How did you manage to do this without being recognized? I thought everyone in town has seen you and Nick in the papers."

"She obviously hadn't. I did a little play-acting, of course."

"Like what?" asked Walter. Carter suddenly remembered this approach was right up Walter's alley. He was a whiz at pretending to be selling vacuums or running a contest to get someone to talk to him without revealing he was a P.I.

"I talked like some of the people I grew up around used to talk. Kinda folksy, but not ignorant."

Sam nodded. "I can see that."

"Then I went to the Californian at Taylor and O'Farrell and got a room for a couple of weeks as Howard T. Albertson from Atlanta visiting a sick friend and also here to see the sights."

Sam chuckled as Walter nodded and said, "Great idea."

"What about luggage?" asked Sam.

"I told them I'd left it at the Southern Pacific depot and would bring it in later."

"Did you?"

"No, why?"

With a big sigh, Sam said, "If you're gonna adopt a persona, you need to fill in all the details." He frowned a little and looked at Walter.

"I've got that old porter's uniform at the office," said Walter. "I can take a cab over there and drop off some luggage at the front desk."

"Why?" asked Carter.

"You can't go back now and walk in with luggage," replied Sam. "If Walter goes over, he can tell them they found your lost bags."

Walter was eagerly nodding. "Of course, you'll have to go over there this afternoon and pick up your luggage from the front desk—"

"Or at least ask about it," said Sam. He looked at Carter. "Did you make the bed looked slept in yesterday?"

Carter shook his head.

"Damn," whispered Sam.

Walter said, "The maids always talk about things like that."

"You didn't pay in advance by any chance?" asked Sam.

"No."

He sighed again. "That's gonna make them really

suspicious. No one slept in the bed and there's no luggage..." He looked up at the ceiling.

Walter said, "What about if you got in a fight last night and ended up in jail? Is Mr. Albertson prone to hooliganism?"

Carter grinned. "He could be." Then he snapped his fingers. "The sick friend."

Nodding, Sam said, "Yeah. Your friend took a turn and you ended up staying overnight at the hospital. Perfect."

"How do we get the bags downstairs without anyone seeing?" asked Carter.

Sam frowned. "Does Nick have any idea about any of this?"

"No," replied Carter.

"Why?" asked Walter in his squeaky voice.

"I don't know..."

"I think I do," said Sam.

"You do?"

"Sure. You think something bad is coming down and you don't want Nick to be hit with it if it's not necessary." He got a wistful expression on his face. "You really love him, don't you?"

"I do. More than anyone or anything I can name."

Walter sighed. "That's so romantic."

"Well," said Sam, "I don't see why Nick needs to know about any of this. If the three of us can figure out what this is about without bothering him, then all the better, doncha think?"

Carter looked down at the parquet pattern on the floor.

"Or we can tell him," said Sam after a long moment.

"I don't know," said Carter. "We don't keep secrets from each other."

"Well, there's secrets and then there's secrets. It's

not like you're hiding the fact that you're secretly boffing Walter, here."

Carter looked over at Sam. "Cut that out." He then glanced at Walter who was just as red as he could be.

"Sorry 'bout that," said Sam.

There was a very uncomfortable pause. Then Carter said, "The truth is that I have a hunch that it's something bad." He looked at Sam. "And you're right... If we can nip this in the bud without having to bother Nick, that would be my druthers." Carter remembered he was the boss. In spite of the fact that Sam and Walter felt completely comfortable speaking their minds, he was still the one in charge. So, in light of that fact, he said, "Walter? Are you OK with keeping this a secret from Nick?"

Walter, who seemed to have recovered from what Sam had said, nodded. "Sure."

Carter looked over at Sam. "What about you?"

"Definitely." Sam then glanced at Walter. "But what about Big Boss?"

"Big Boss?" asked Carter. "Who's that?"

"Mr. Robertson," squeaked Walter. He was talking about Mike.

Carter laughed. "Makes sense. He's taller than me."

Walter glanced at Sam who said, "More importantly, he's made it clear he's in charge."

"And he is," said Carter.

"He's, uh, very *adamant* about that," added Walter as he pushed his glasses up his nose.

"Good," said Carter.

With a big grin, Sam said, "He's gonna wipe the floor with all our asses if he finds out we're doing anything behind his back."

Carter nodded. "I know. So, I guess that means we have to make sure he doesn't find out about any of this." He looked at Walter. "So, that also means no one outside of this room finds out about what we're doing. OK?"

Walter nodded. "Yes, sir."

Carter looked at Sam. "And I know I don't have to worry about you. You must be creamin' your shorts gettin' my permission to keep a secret from Mike."

Walter honked out a laugh as Sam offered up a big smile, wiggled his eyebrows, and replied, "No more than you are."

Carter nodded since Sam wasn't wrong about that.

. . .

"Where've you been, Chief?" asked Nick as Carter walked past him so he could get a glass of Burgie beer from Gustav who was manning the bar.

With a smile, Carter replied, "Chewin' the fat with Sam and Walter."

"Oh?" asked Nick with a slight frown.

Out of the corner of his eye, Carter saw that Marnie was standing by the door to the back garden and signaling him. "Yes, Sam was telling us a story about a soldier who was guarding Stalin one time."

Nick guffawed. "That's one of my *favorite* stories."

Carter forced himself to laugh and nod. "Mine, too." He subtly pointed to the garden door. "I think your father is looking for me." He put his hand on Nick's shoulder and squeezed. "Be back in a bit."

"Sure," replied Nick as Robert walked up and said, "I'm stuffed!"

. . .

Carter followed Marnie over to the bench next to the back wall. Dr. Williams was standing near the door to the house and chatting with Lettie (Marnie's mother),

Louise (Carter's mother), and Velma (her sister) about a story he'd read in the *Examiner* about the smog down in L.A.

"What is it?" asked Carter as he looked down at Marnie and smiled.

She turned so that no one else could see her. In a quiet voice, she said, "There were two men yesterday who came to the office asking about Nick."

Carter just nodded.

She continued, "This was the second time they've come by and this time they kinda scared me."

"What'd they do?"

She crossed her arms. "Well, the one—I think he was with the government—or that's what he said. He told me that Nick was gonna be in trouble if he didn't stop hiding out." She looked up at him with worry all over her face. "What kinda trouble? What's goin' on, Carter?"

He smiled reassuringly. "Nick's not in any more trouble than he usually his." That apparently didn't make her feel better, so he added, "What I mean is that, you know, the F.B.I. is always watching us. Just like the cops."

She nodded. "I know, but this was different, somehow." She shrugged. "And then there was the other guy."

"What did he do?"

"He just stood there and stared at me. It was like he was lookin' right through me. It was scary."

Carter touched her shoulder. "Next time you see them, come get me."

Her eyes widened a bit. "Should I talk to Nick?"

Taking a deep breath, Carter replied, "Of course. But what will you tell him, exactly?" He was beginning to feel like a real heel.

Shouldn't I be telling Marnie what I know?

Before he could do or say anything, one way or another, Sam was at his elbow. "Pardon me, Marnie. Can I borrow this big guy for a minute?"

She nodded. "Sure." She looked up at Carter.

"Don't worry," he said.

She nodded again and wandered over to join Dr. Williams and the ladies.

"What was that about?" hissed Sam.

"She said those guys have talked to her twice."

"When?"

"Yesterday and one other time."

"You really need to dig for details if you're gonna do the private dick thing."

Carter felt his hand rise up to rub his chin. He was getting angry and that was his body's way of letting him know. He forced it down. He quietly, but firmly, said, "I didn't get that far. You interrupted me."

"Looked to me as if you were about to spill the beans."

"You don't think we should tell Marnie?"

"I was thinkin' about our pow-wow in your office just now and realized you were right. We need to keep this just between the three of us."

"You two look like you're plotting something," crowed Henry as he walked up. "Thick as thieves!" He seemed to be in a good mood, which was a relief to Carter who'd been avoiding him all day. He didn't want to hear any of his complaints about Robert.

Sam turned and grinned at Henry. He reached over and quickly yanked on Henry's brown and yellow tie and then let go. That all happened in a flash. He whispered, "I think you're even more handsome than your *doppelganger*, Mr. Henry Winters."

With a blush, Henry turned on his heels and fled back into the house. Carter noticed his mother was frowning at him. Looking down at Sam, he hissed, "You can be such an ass sometimes."

Sam nodded with a satisfied grin. "I know and I know Henry can dish it out ten times worse than me." He looked over his shoulder at the back door and then up at Carter. "Robert and Marnie hold your company together and I don't like it when anyone—*anyone*—fucks with either of 'em." Sam stalked into the house.

Carter didn't want to condone Sam's behavior, but he also didn't disagree with what he'd just said. With that on his mind, Carter ambled back towards the door, smiling at Dr. Williams and the ladies, who were still talking about how terrible the smog was down in L.A.

He was halfway to the bar (and that much needed glass of Burgie) when he heard his mother clear her throat behind him. Taking a deep breath, Carter turned around and looked down at her with a plastered-on smile. "Wasn't Mrs. Strakova's roast turkey really good? Almost as good as yours, but not quite."

His mother shook her head a little and whispered, "Carter Jones, don't you try and flim-flam me."

"Yes, ma'am."

"What was all that about between you and Henry and Mr. Halversen?"

"Nothing, Mama."

"That was not nothing." She crossed her arms. "I swear I just don't like Mr. Halversen." She glanced over at where Sam was quietly talking with Gustav. "He's like a lion among the lambs."

"Now, Mama..."

She sniffed. "And another thing. Were you aware that two strange men came knocking on Leticia's door yesterday asking for Nick?"

Why is she repeating what Dr. Williams just told me?

Regardless of why, Carter definitely knew better

than to let her know he was aware of what was going on, so he said, "Who were they?"

"Leticia didn't know and she asked me to talk to you because Parnell doesn't want to bother Nicholas with any of this."

Carter couldn't imagine that Dr. Williams had actually said anything like that, but he asked, "Did she mention what they asked?"

"The man from the government said that Nicholas needs to stop, and I quote, 'dodging him'. Can you imagine?" She shook her head. "And after all the taxes you two pay. Why can't the government just leave you alone?"

"Did Lettie mention anything about the other man?"

"She said he was foreign even though his English was perfect."

Carter nodded.

"Back to Henry. I've been writing to his mother."

That alarmed Carter. "No, Mama, don't."

"Well, a lot of good it's doing since she hasn't once had the courtesy to reply."

"You know there's a lot of bad blood there." He lowered his voice. "When we were in Albany last year, he never told any of his family."

"I know that," snapped his mother in reply. "That's why I started writing to her." She sighed and softened a bit. "It was Leticia's idea, to be honest. Velma and I wouldn't be here if it weren't for her."

Carter smiled. "I know, Mama, and I'm glad you're here."

She reached over and touched his arm. "Me, too, son. Me, too."

. . .

Carter finally got his glass of Burgie and was headed over to the fireplace to check on the fire and talk to Robert when he saw that Sam was standing next to the front door and pointing at the office by jerking his head to the side a little. After looking around to find Nick and then remembering he'd walked outside while Carter had been talking to his mother, he made his way towards office and followed Sam inside.

Walter was already there and, once again, standing by the trophy case.

As Sam closed the door, Carter sat down in his chair and said, "No fewer than four people have told me that Bonnist and Sladek have been looking for Nick."

"Who?" asked Walter.

"Dr. Williams, Mr. LeBeau, Marnie, and my mother. And all of them feel the same way we do. They don't want to talk to Nick about it." He looked over at Sam and asked, "What's up?"

"Something is really bothering Gustav," said Sam.

Walter nodded. "And Ferdinand."

"How do you know that?"

"Anna"—he was talking about Mrs. Kopek—"pulled me aside and said they were arguing last night and again this morning."

Carter nodded. One thing he absolutely hated about the layout of the house was that all the staff—all six of them—were crammed into monk-like cells under the kitchen and all shared one bathroom that only had a bathtub and no shower. When he'd asked Mrs. Kopek about the layout, she'd just smiled and said that it was fine. Carter and Nick had talked about building out a couple of bedrooms in the attic—one for Gustav and Ferdinand and one for Ida and Nora—but that idea had been shot down by everyone concerned. Apparently, they all enjoyed living down there. Carter didn't

68

understand why, particularly in the case of Mrs. Kopek who, when they'd met her a year earlier, had been living in her own apartment with her now-deceased husband. But that would explain why she knew about Gustav and Ferdinand arguing. Carter asked, "Did she mention what they were arguing about?"

"Something about a man they both knew back in Prague."

Carter frowned. "This is obviously connected to Alexander Sladek."

"Maybe," said Sam. "I asked her if they mentioned a name and she said they didn't. They just kept talking about some man. She did say that Ferdinand was the one who was angry, and that Gustav was trying to calm him down."

Walter added, "I had a hunch about this."

"You did?" asked Carter.

"Well, yes. It seemed obvious. This Sladek person is Czechoslovakian." He put out his hands for emphasis. "And *they're* Czechoslovakian."

"But so are the rest."

"Anna is really Polish," offered Sam. "But, yeah, you're right. For all intents and purposes, they're all Czech."

Walter tilted his head. "Why not say the whole word?"

Sam grinned. "Because Gustav, Ferdinand, Ida, Nora, and Mrs. Strakova are all Czechs. Anna is Silesian Polish but was born in the same part of the Austrian Empire, like Mrs. Strakova and myself, that became what is now Czechoslovakia but, theoretically, could have just as easily been made part of Poland after the Great War. As far as Czechs are concerned, we don't have enough time for me to explain all the distinctions between the Bohemians, Moravians, and Silesians and compare all of them to all the different kinds of Slovaks. But believe me, though, if you ever meet a Slovak, do *not* call him a Czech."

Walter glanced at Carter. "OK."

Carter chuckled. "Glad we got that cleared up."

"But the first thing we need to do is get some luggage over to your room at the Californian," said Sam.

Carter stood. "You're right. I'll bring down a couple of empty valises and—"

Walter clicked his tongue as Sam said, "No good. They need to have clothes in them in case someone rifles through your stuff."

"And you should unpack them," added Walter.

"Oh, right," said Carter. He sighed. "And I do need to show up since I might have a message waiting for me there from David Bonnist."

Looking up at him, Walter peered through his big glasses and quietly said, "Or a message for Howard T. Albertson from David Bonnist."

Carter resisted the urge to pat Walter on the head. Instead, he said, "Exactly."

. . .

At the top of the stairs, Carter found Marnie and Alex coming down from the third floor.

"Oh, Carter!" exclaimed Marnie, blushing and straightening her skirt.

Carter grinned just a little because he couldn't help it. Her hair was a little out of place and her lipstick was smudged while Alex had some of the her lipstick on one side of his mouth.

"Sorry for the intrusion," said Alex, looking a little nervous.

"Alex had never seen the third floor and all those cute bedrooms Nick's mother designed before..." She

70

frowned.

"Before she died," said Carter, completing the thought for her.

She nodded.

"What's the story there?" asked Alex.

"Nick's mother had cancer and left to die in Mexico." Carter thought the question was rude and was pretty sure the tone of his voice reflected that feeling when he replied.

"I just wondered because Nick never really talks about her. My parents—"

"Will y'all excuse me?" said Carter as he stepped around Marnie. "I need to get something for Dr. Williams out of our bathroom and he's waiting for me."

"Oh, sure," said Marnie.

As Carter made his way down the hall, he could hear Alex asking, "What? Did I say the wrong thing?"

"I told you not to bring her up," was Marnie's reply as they walked downstairs.

. . .

Once he had a couple of valises packed with some of the older clothes he didn't much wear anymore, Carter wondered how to sneak them out without letting anyone, particularly Nick, see him or them.

He was staring at the valises, trying to figure out what to do next, when he heard a knock on the door. "Mr. Jones?" It was Walter.

"Come in," replied Carter, feeling relieved. Walter always had a plan.

The door pushed open a few inches and Walter squeezed through the tiny opening he'd made for himself. Eyes wider than Carter had ever seen them, he looked around the room. "Golly," he whispered to himself.

"Have you never been in here?"

Walter shook his head as he stood by the door.

"It's amazing, right?" asked Carter.

Walter nodded.

Pointing to the ceiling, Carter said, "Look at that."

"Wow!" said Walter as he stared. "That's just like the ceiling downstairs in the office."

"Dr. Williams told me that, according to his father, all the rooms had carved ceilings like this before the fire. After that, Michael Williams—Nick's grandfather—had the same artists carve just the ceilings for this room and the office."

"Wow..." Walter walked into the room.

Carter noticed that he was ignoring the bed and that seemed to be on purpose. So, he decided to skip his story about who made the bed and how durable it was. Instead, he pointed at the valises. "What should I do with these?"

Walter walked over to the window that looked out at Grace Cathedral. "Does this open?"

"Sure." Carter walked over and slid open the bottom sash.

Walter got right next to Carter and stuck his head outside. "I'll go down there, and you can drop them down to me."

"Are you sure?"

Nodding, Walter said, "It's only fifteen feet at the most to the sidewalk."

"What if someone sees us?"

Walter looked up and, as if he'd just realized he was standing right next to Carter, he hastily beat a retreat to the Chesterfield sofa between the bed and the fireplace where he stammered, "It's, uh, Thanksgiving Day, Mr. Jones. Right?" He laughed nervously. Before Carter could reply, Walter made a beeline for the door, saying,

"I'll see you in a minute," as he fled down the hallway.

Carter just shook his head.

. . .

Carter was heading downstairs when Sam popped out of the office. They met in front of the door and Sam whispered, "Where's Walter?"

"I tossed the valises out of our bedroom window and Walter grabbed them. He walked over to California and caught a cab."

Sam nodded. Then he looked up at Carter. "I saw him going upstairs. Did he have a heart attack when he saw that big bed of yours?"

"What do you mean?"

Sam grinned. "You know the poor kid wants nothing more than to be the bologna in a Carter and Mike sandwich, right?"

"I didn't," replied Carter, stiffly. He saw Nick talking to his mother over by the redwood dining table and headed in that direction. For once, the thought of being caught in a conversation with his mother was a relief. At least she wouldn't bring up uncomfortable subjects like Sam always did. He could count on that.

. . .

After most everyone had left, Mike and his lover, Greg Holland, showed up. That was around half past 6. Henry and Robert were the only ones left from the lunch crowd, although Henry was upstairs in Nick's old bedroom, having a nap.

As Nick handed out tumblers of whiskey to Mike and Greg, Robert asked, "Did you two have Thanksgiving dinner at home?"

Mike, who was lighting his cigar, stopped long enough to say, "We were supposed to have dinner at the Palace."

"But someone forgot to make a reservation," said Greg.

Mike rolled his eyes. "Someone named Gregory Alan Holland."

"We ended up at Moar's."

"A *cafeteria*?" asked Robert, sounding offended.

Greg nodded.

"Actually, I had the roast beef," said Mike after puffing on his cigar. "And it was about the best I've ever had."

"I had the turkey. Really juicy."

Carter watched as Nick crossed his legs (he was sitting on one of the chairs from the dining table) and made a face. "I wish you two would have joined us. We had plenty of food."

Mike shook his head. He looked at the ash end of his cigar and said, "I'm not ready to spend that much time with your father and I'd guess he feels the same."

"You might be surprised," said Carter, thinking about how much Dr. Williams had changed since he'd met and married Lettie.

"I *would* be surprised," said Mike. "Very."

"I originally wanted to go to the Claremont," said Greg. "But they didn't start serving until 3."

"In Berkeley?" asked Robert as if Greg was talking about Timbuktu.

"Have you ever been there?" asked Greg. "When I was married to Doris, we used to take the Key train over and spend the day walking around when I had a weekday off."

"Speaking of that," said Robert, "did any of you go to the World's Fair on Treasure Island?"

Everyone nodded.

Mike said, "I took Nick."

"I took Henry," said Carter. "Well, actually, he and I met there. He took the Key train from Cal." He grinned and looked over at Robert. "Did he tell you about the two gals he brought with him?"

"No," said Robert a little stiffly. "I had no idea he'd been there."

"You should ask him some time. It's a funny story."

"What's a funny story?" asked Henry who was walking down the stairs right then.

Robert replied, "The time you and Carter went to the World's Fair on Treasure Island."

Wiping the sleep out of his eyes, Henry snorted. "That was a dud of an adventure."

"How so?" asked Nick.

Henry sat on the arm of Robert's chair. "I was supposed to meet Carter there after classes were over. I took the train and met up with this one girl I really liked but she was with her sister or cousin..." He looked at Carter.

"Cat James was the one you liked," said Carter since he rarely forgot a name, "and Mary Margaret Maxwell was her second cousin from Chicago."

"Right," said Henry with a nod. "Anyway, Cat was apologetic, but this Mary Margaret was a real pest. We tried to get into this nice French restaurant but the man there was real snooty and even kept the tip I gave him so we could get a table."

"They were full, Henry. He couldn't magically make a table appear."

Henry rolled his eyes. "Anyway, Carter and I ended up grabbing a hot dog and sitting on the benches that looked across the bay at Oakland." He shrugged. "It was a nice night in the end."

Nick leaned forward. "How much was the tip you gave him?"

"A whole buck! And, you know, I was in college at the time and that was a lotta money."

Nick was smiling by then. He looked over at Mike. "Do you remember this? That maitre d' who wanted you to arrest me because I was asking for my dollar back?

Mike looked at Henry and then at Nick. He burst out laughing as he pointed at Henry with his cigar. "You nearly got Nick busted that night. That guy was really angry."

"What do you mean?" asked Henry with a frown creasing his forehead.

"What I mean is that we musta all been there the same night." Mike looked over at Carter. "Columbus Day? 1940?"

Carter nodded. "That was it."

Mike laughed again. "I always wondered what the hell that man was so upset about and now I know."

"What *are* you talking about?" asked Henry.

With his free hand, Mike drew a line down his cheek. "Before that German officer gave you that souvenir, you musta looked just like Nick."

"That's ridiculous," said Nick. "Everyone knows Henry is much more handsome than me."

Everyone but Henry laughed at that.

Carter said, "That must be what happened. Because the guy at the French restaurant was really steamed when we left."

Henry stood up. "I think it's time for us to leave." He looked down at Robert.

"Aw, Henry," said Mike. "Doncha think it's funny that we were all there on the same night? I think it's kinda sweet." He glanced over at Carter and winked.

That was when a long-forgotten memory surfaced in Carter's mind. He pointed at Mike. "We saw you."

"You did?"

Carter nodded. "Henry and I were on our way back to the ferry and leaving the Redwood Pavilion and walked right past you." He sat back, surprised. "I saw you." Then he looked at Nick. "But I didn't see you since it was dark." He turned back to Mike. "We even nodded at each other."

"We did?" said Mike before taking a sip of his whiskey. "I don't remember. But, then again, the only thing I remember about that day is how mad that French guy was when Nick walked up and asked for a table."

"Robert!" barked Henry as he stalked over to the front door. "Are you coming?"

. . .

As usual, Carter had mixed feelings after Henry and Robert left. On the one hand, it was a relief to not have to deal with all of Henry's many moods. On the other hand, Carter still loved Henry. And Robert. And he knew that Nick loved Henry and liked him much more than Carter did.

In any event, he didn't get much of a chance to mull any of that over because, about two minutes after Henry ran out with an apologetic Robert following him, the phone rang.

Mike was saying, "What I most remember about all that over on Treasure Island was when I pulled a few weeks patrol and had to listen to the barker who was hawking Sally Rand's nude ranch over and over again," when Gustav appeared at Carter's arm, leaned over, and whispered, "It is Sam for you on the telephone."

Carter stood, said, "Excuse me," and then followed Gustav into the kitchen.

. . .

"Hi, Sam." Carter was talking on the new extension on the back wall of the kitchen. He was alone and the place looked and smelled clean.

"This is your friendly reminder that Howard T. Albertson needs to put in an appearance at the Hotel Californian."

"I know. I just haven't been able to figure out how to get out of here without it looking suspicious."

Sam laughed. "You really are such a juvenile when it comes to being a private dick."

Ignoring that, Carter asked, "Any suggestions?"

"Just tell Nick you have to go to Sugar Joe's."

"But Mike and Greg are here."

Sam was quiet for a moment. "I got it. Go tell them that I just called from Sugar Joe's and that there's a problem and Joe needs your help."

"What kinda problem and what kinda help?"

Sam huffed into the phone. "You want me to hold your hand?" Sam's American accent was slipping.

"You're the master, Sam. I am but the student."

With a guffaw, Sam said, "Now you're talkin'. Gimme a sec and I'll come up with the perfect plan."

Carter grinned to himself. Sam's American accent was back.

"Well..." Carter heard him snap his fingers. "Got it. Sugar Joe called you 'cause he just got a notice from the Internal Revenue Bureau and needs your help."

Carter nodded. "That's not unreasonable."

"Get to it, bud." Sam laughed to himself. "You called me the master. I'll remember that."

Before Carter could reply to that, the line went dead.

. . .

78

"Who was it?" asked Nick as Carter walked back into the great room.

"Sugar Joe. He got a tax notice and wants my advice. Do y'all mind if I duck out for an hour or so?"

Mike looked over. "Tax notice? On Thanksgiving?"

"He got it a couple of days ago and just realized he hadn't called me."

Mike frowned a little and then shrugged. He looked at Nick. "Should we go?"

"You two stay and keep me company."

Greg turned to look at Carter. "I know you two had a big lunch, but how about meeting us at the Far East for dinner?" He looked at his watch and then at Nick. "It's almost 6. What if we plan on heading over there at half past 7?"

Nick smiled. "Sounds good." Looking at Carter, he asked, "That give you enough time?"

"Sure," replied Carter with a smile on the outside and the crushing feeling of having betrayed Nick on the inside.

. . .

Carter was in the kitchen and about to head down to the garage. He'd just put his hand on the doorknob when he heard Ferdinand say, "Mr. Carter?"

He stopped and turned around. "Yes?"

"Where you go?"

"Sugar Joe's," lied Carter.

Ferdinand looked him up and down. "Wrong clothes, I think."

Carter chuckled. "I'm not going to lift weights. I'm going to talk to Joe."

The other man nodded and then said, "I talk to you later, no?"

"Sure," said Carter.

Ferdinand nodded, turned, and jogged back down the stairs to the room that he shared with Gustav.

Chapter 5: Mr. Albertson checks in.

Hotel Californian
Corner of O'Farrell and Taylor
San Francisco, Cal.
Thursday, November 25, 1954
Just past 6 in the evening

Carter was pulling into the garage on Mason that was next to the Hotel Californian when he suddenly realized the opportunity he'd missed. As he handed the keys to the attendant and gave him a five to keep it out instead of parking it, Carter was chastising himself for not taking Ferdinand with him so they could talk alone. Walter was right. Sladek, the man from the Czechoslovakian Consulate in New York, had to be somehow connected to Gustav and Ferdinand. Carter just couldn't imagine why until he was pushing his way through the hotel's revolving door.

It suddenly hit him—and hard—like one of

Ferdinand's fists making contact with his kidney when they would box at Sugar Joe's. Maybe Sladek was trying to, somehow, get Gustav and Ferdinand to go back to Czechoslovakia.

Walking across the lobby, Carter knew neither man wanted to go back. They'd said as much when they'd first come to work for him and Nick.

"Ah, Mr. Albertson," said a man's voice, bringing Carter out of his musing.

"Why, you're the very man who checked me in yesterday, aren't you?"

"Yes, sir. We were concerned when you left and never returned."

Carter took off his hat and pressed it against his chest. "Well, I'm so sorry about that. You see, when I went to see my friend in the hospital, he'd taken a turn for the worse and I ended up spendin' the night there."

"I see. Well, a porter from the Southern Pacific depot was here not half an hour ago and dropped off your two valises."

Carter grinned. "Well, wasn't that friendly of him? I called over there and asked them if they might do that."

The man arched an eyebrow at Carter. "He said your luggage had been lost."

Shit.

"Well, yes," said Carter. He cleared his throat. "They *were* lost, but now they found them. And isn't that a nice thing for them to bring them all the way here?"

"Yes."

Carter smiled as big as he could. "Well, thank you for lettin' me know. Are they upstairs or do I need to go and get 'em somewhere?"

"They're in your room, Mr. Alexander."

"Thank you, kindly." Carter started to walk away.

"Mr. Alexander?" called out the man.

Carter turned. "Yes?"

"The management of the hotel would like to obtain payment up front. If you don't mind."

Walking back over to the desk, Carter grinned. "Not at all." He pulled out his wallet and handed the man a hundred. "Will that do?"

The man blinked a couple of times. "Of course. One moment and I'll write out a receipt."

Carter just smiled at the man as he waited.

. . .

Once up in his room, Carter decided to do what Walter had suggested. He unpacked his bags so the room would look lived in. Once he had everything put up and hung up, he stashed the bags in the corner.

He then kicked off his shoes and took off his coat. Pulling down the covers of the single bed, he climbed in and rolled around on it a little.

Once he was satisfied the bed looked slept-in, he sat up and reached over for his shoes. He was untying the first one when the phone rang.

He dropped his shoe on the floor and reached over for the receiver. "Hello?"

"Is this Howard Albertson?" asked a man's voice.

"Speakin'."

"This is David Bonnist. My secretary told me you stopped in yesterday. Is there something I can help you with?"

Carter panicked for a moment. He had almost forgotten he'd asked Miss Owens to have her boss call him.

"Mr. Albertson? Are you there?"

"Why, sure. My apologies, Mr. Bonnist. I had something stuck in my throat."

"Should I call back later?"

"Oh, no! No! Thank you for callin',"

"I understand you might be having some sort of trouble that I can help you with?"

"Yes..."

But what?

Carter's mind raced as he tried to remember all the cases Nick had ever told him about or that he'd heard about from Mike or any of their other employees.

"Mr. Albertson?"

"I beg your pardon. I guess you could say this is a sensitive subject."

"What is?"

"Well..." Carter looked over at the bedside table and he saw a book of matches with the hotel's name printed on it. "Matches," he said, more to himself than to the man on the phone. To cover his embarrassment, Carter coughed.

"Matches?"

"Why, yes." Carter shifted around a little. Like the sun rising over the ocean, an idea for a story was coming to him. But it wasn't quite formed. Not yet.

"What about matches?"

"Well, you see, I'm here in town visitin' a friend who's in the hospital. We went to Emory University together back home in Atlanta. Which is where I'm from."

"I see."

"And my friend... Well, you see, he's not doin' well, and he has a problem."

"What kind of problem?"

"His wife..."

"His wife?"

"Yes," said Carter before clearing his throat again. "His wife may be steppin' out on him and my friend

84

thinks that this fella she's steppin' out with is from someplace like Czechoslovakia or maybe Yugoslavia or someplace like that and I met this other fella on the train up here from Los Angeles who gave me your name and said you might be just the man to help me."

"What was *his* name?"

Carter knew he was asking about the man on the train, but he decided to act dumb. "The foreign man? I couldn't tell you. That's why I'm callin' you."

Bonnist chuckled. "Of course. What, exactly, can I do for you?"

"Well, it's not so much *for me* as it is for my friend, who really might not make it through the weekend and who's never really had what you might call a strong constitution."

"I'm sorry to hear that. What's his name?"

Carter froze.

"Mr. Albertson?"

"Well, sir..."

"I understand if you wish to keep his name confidential although if this is about doing an undercover job to see if his wife is being unfaithful, I will have to know her name. And finding out his name will become a foregone conclusion, if you follow me." Carter suddenly realized the way the man talked reminded him of all the cops he worked with. He wondered if Bonnist had ever been on the police force in San Francisco or somewhere else. His accent was a little fancier than Mike's, though, which made Carter think the man might be from somewhere back east.

"Mr. Albertson? Hello?"

"My apologies, sir. I'm still here." Carter took a deep breath. "I guess neither one of us—my friend and me, I mean... Neither one of us thought this through very well."

85

"Of course." Bonnist was losing interest. Carter didn't blame the man. He was making Howard T. Albertson sound like a nut.

Pulling himself together, Carter asked, "Do you mind if I call my friend and ask him what he wants to do? I'm just the go-between, doncha know?"

"Certainly. You can always call my office. I'll be in for another hour or so. After that, you can leave a message with the service."

"Well, thank you, kindly. I sure appreciate your help."

"My pleasure, Mr. Albertson. I'll look forward to speaking with you again, soon."

"Goodbye."

"Goodbye, Mr. Albertson."

Carter put the receiver down and thought for a moment. Then he picked it back up and waited.

"Operator. How may I help you?"

"I need to make a local call, but I don't know the number."

"What's the name?"

"Samuel Halversen."

"One moment."

He waited as he heard her paging through the phone book. After a moment, she said, "I have it here. Do you want the telephone number before I connect you?"

"Yes, ma'am." Carter reached for the pencil and pad next to the phone.

"It's Yukon 6-5593."

Carter repeated the number back to her.

"Correct. I'll connect you now."

"Thank you, ma'am."

"My pleasure."

After a moment, Carter heard a click and then the line started ringing.

"Hello?"

"Sam? It's Carter."

"Hi, there. What can I do you for?"

"I'm at the hotel. Bonnist just called."

"Hot damn! What happened?"

Carter repeated the conversation as best as he could.

"So, he's at his office?"

"Yes."

"I say we go down there and corner him."

"Are you sure?"

"Sure. We'll have the element of surprise on our side. We can corner him and find out what he's up to with this Sladek."

"Ferdinand wants to talk to me when I get back. I think he wants to tell me what he and Gustav were fighting about." Carter faltered a little. "That's just a hunch, really."

"Hmm..."

"Should we talk to him first and then go to Bonnist?"

Sam took a deep breath. "Nah. Let's hit Bonnist first."

"Fine. You wanna meet me there?"

"Come pick me up. I'm on the way."

"I thought you and Ike lived together up in North Beach."

"We do. But I'm at my place."

"Your place?"

"My apartment."

Carter didn't understand why he would have two apartments, but he didn't really care. That was the sort of thing that would have bothered Nick who would have immediately pounced on Sam and interrogated him without waiting. But Carter figured Sam would tell him in his own sweet time. He asked, "What's the address?"

"432 Jessie. You know where that is?"

Carter was surprised. "Of course. By Truck Company number 1 and Engine 17."

"Around the corner, but that's it."

"I didn't think anyone lived over there."

Sam just laughed and said, "I'll be waitin' for ya, sailor."

Chapter 6: Picking up Sam.

432 Jessie Street
San Francisco, Cal.
Thursday, November 25, 1954
A quarter before 7 in the evening

When he got down there, Carter peered into the darkness but didn't see a number plate for 432, which was odd considering the fact that a fire station was just a few feet away. Jessie was a two-way street with no room for parking, so Carter did what most people did on alleys South of the Slot and parked up on the sidewalk. Wobber Brothers printing and stationery plant was at 444 and was closed for the holiday (per the sign on their door). He parked in front of their empty loading dock and waited for Sam to appear.

The area was deserted except for a small handful of tourists having a look at the old Mint, which was the building that made Jessie curve around on its way from 5th Street to 6th. The firehouse, in fact, was located where it was in order to protect the mint which was at least 60 years old, if not older. It had survived the earthquake and the fire because of the fact that it was built out of stone and had an interior courtyard. Or that was the story Carter had always heard. The government had opened the new Mint right before Carter moved to the City and that was on Market, just this side of Eureka Valley and at the top of Dolores Street.

Sam suddenly pushed his way through a door Carter hadn't noticed until it opened. It was painted the same dull brown as the rest of the Wobber Brothers building.

Grinning, Sam opened the passenger door and hopped in. "Fancy meeting you here, sailor."

Carter put the car in gear and drove onto the street. "Where is your apartment?"

"It's behind the loading dock and once belonged to the plant foreman who used to live onsite before the war and worked for the Wobber brothers. You know either of them?"

"I see William Wobber's name in the papers every now and then. Don't they own a couple of movie theaters with Mr. Curran?"

"Yep," replied Sam as Carter turned right to head south down Mission.

. . .

Carter decided to take Mission down to 17th before moving over to Folsom.

They'd just passed 9th Street when Sam asked, "So, when are you gonna grill me about Ike?"

With a shrug, Carter said, "Probably never. I'm not Nick."

Sam chuckled as he looked out the window. "You sure aren't."

Like he'd done earlier, Carter reminded himself to be

calm and polite. Sam was his employee. And, since he couldn't think of anything nice to say, he kept his mouth closed and focused on driving.

After a few moments, Sam said, "Sorry about that. It came out the wrong way." He looked over at Carter. "What I meant to say is that I know you're more easy-going than Nick or Mike and I appreciate that. A lot of us guys feel the same way."

Carter didn't know how to reply, so he decided to do what Nick always did in situations like that. He would wait and let whoever was talking just keep talking. It was a nifty trick. Besides, Carter was sure Sam had more he wanted to say.

"I love Ike," said Sam about the time they passed under the green light at 16th Street.

Carter turned on his left blinker and also stuck his arm out the window to indicate they would be making a turn at 17th Street. He also said, "I know you do."

"But we have problems."

The oncoming traffic was light, so Carter made a left onto 17th and proceeded towards South Van Ness.

"I think I'm too old for him."

Carter wanted to mention how Ike's father had passed away right before the time they got together, and that Sam was the same age as the man, and how that meant that Ike might be in love with Ike as a father-figure, not a lover, but he didn't.

"And he's involved in something that's probably illegal, but I don't know what it is."

"Have you talked to Mike or Nick about that?" asked Carter as he put out his arm to indicate he was about to turn right on Folsom.

Sam snorted. "Mike's a cop and Nick might as well be one."

Carter glanced over. Sam was staring out the

passenger window. "Is that what you meant earlier about how I'm not the same as Nick and Mike?"

"Yeah."

By that time, Carter was trying to figure out where to park. That block of Folsom was industrial and, therefore, had plenty of open spaces on both sides.

"Park right here," said Sam, as if he was reading Carter's mind.

. . .

Sam pointed through the windshield. "I see there's a party at the motorcycle club."

Carter nodded. Even with the windows rolled up, he could hear some kind of music being played over a jukebox.

"They must have a window open," said Sam.

"Do you know that song?"

"Sure. It's 'Cry, Cry Darling'." He chuckled and shifted in his seat. "It's one of Ike's favorite songs."

"Ike likes that hillbilly stuff?"

"Hillbilly?" asked Sam. "Don't they have music like that where you're from?"

"I have no idea," replied Carter. He looked at his watch but couldn't see what time it was. He quickly switched the dashboard on and off. It was 7:20. "Shit," he muttered to himself.

"Got somewhere to be?"

"The Far East in ten minutes."

Sam laughed. "Sorry, but you're gonna be late."

"I should call Nick."

"There's probably a payphone over on Mission." Sam sighed. "Why didn't you tell me you were on a schedule? We could have done this differently if I'd known that."

"I forgot."

Sam turned to stare at him. "You never forget anything."

Carter shrugged. Sam was right, though. He never forgot anything. The truth was that Carter was out of his element. He felt like he was a blind man walking around and having to make his way by feeling things. It was disorienting to say the least. He was about to explain that to Sam when he saw a man step out onto the sidewalk from Bonnist's office. A light from the plastic factory hit his face just right. It was definitely the American man who'd shown up at the front door on Wednesday morning. He turned around to lock the door with a key. "Look," hissed Carter as he pointed. "That's him, isn't it?"

Sam nodded. "Yep. That's David Bonnist, alright. Let's watch what he does before we make a move."

Bonnist immediately started heading down the sidewalk towards where they were parked.

Sam quickly leaned over and put his head in Carter's lap causing Carter to grunt in surprise. Sam whispered, "Pull your hat down and keep your eyes open but try to look like you're asleep or getting a blow job." He quietly chuckled.

As he yanked his hat down over his forehead, Carter whispered back, "I bet other private eyes don't pretend to be giving blow jobs on stake-outs."

"You'd be surprised. What's he doing?"

"He's about to walk by us."

"Watch him but don't let him know you're watching him."

"He's just pulled out a cigarette to light it." Carter watched the man walk right by the car without looking inside. "He's past us."

"Keep your eyes on the mirrors. Can you see him?"

"Yes. He's making a left at the—" Carter didn't finish

because Sam had quietly opened the door and was sliding out.

"Stay here," he hissed as he walked off without closing the door.

Carter reached over and slowly pulled the door closed until he heard the first click.

. . .

In less than 10 minutes, Sam was back. He opened the door and got in. "Go. He's headed north on Mission in a red Olds 88. A '52, I think."

Carter started up the car and then, after checking both ways, made a U-turn and headed north on Folsom.

"Take 17th over. It's faster."

Carter gritted his teeth. He hated to be given directions on how to drive, particularly in San Francisco. Then he remembered Mike saying that no one knew how to get around the City better than Sam. Nick had agreed with that.

"There won't be any cops around so, if it's safe, you can probably blow a few red lights."

Carter sighed as he made a fast right onto Mission. "Where do you think he's headed?"

"Home."

"Do you know where that is?"

Sam was leaning forward and staring through the windshield. "You can run this red." They were at 16th. "There's no one coming either way."

Carter hesitated.

"Go!" barked Sam, really sounding like Ferdinand. "We'll miss him."

Carter ran the red light, asking, "*Where* are we going?"

"We're going to his house, but I wanna make sure

that's where he goes which is why we're chasing him."

"But where does he live?"

"Slow down." They were coming up to 14th Street and the light was red. Sam leaned forward. "OK. You can go."

Carter gunned the engine and they shot through the intersection. "I think I see an Olds going around the curve."

"That's him. Plate 3R18871. It's a match."

"You can see that far ahead?"

"I have great eyesight," said Sam.

"And a good memory."

"Just like you."

Carter nodded. He slowed down as they approached the Van Ness intersection.

"Look," said Sam. "He's turning left. Just like he should. He's a good boy, goin' home to wifey."

"Should I follow him?"

"Yes, but stay back. It's a good thing it's dark. Otherwise, your car would stick out like a big banana, it's so yellow."

"Oh," said Carter. "I hadn't thought of that."

"Such a juvenile..." muttered Sam.

The light changed and Bonnist made his left in his red Olds. Carter was right behind him but followed slowly so the distance between the cars would increase. "Now, where are we going?" he asked a little more impatiently than he wanted to.

"So, you really don't know who this guy is, do you? That surprises me."

"He's a private eye."

Sam cleared his throat. "He's a private eye, like Nick is a private eye."

"What does that mean?" They were crossing Market with a green light. Carter was moving slow enough that a '49 Chevy was able to change lanes and get in between their two cars.

"That's good," said Sam. "He'll stay in the left lane until we get to California."

"Sam! Tell me who this guy is."

"He's the son-in-law of one of your father-in-law's cronies. Bonnist married the California Amalgamated heiress."

"Deidre Webb?"

"Now Deidre Bonnist. Daughter of Peter Orson Webb, member of the Pacific-Union Club and the Bohemian Club, and close childhood friend of Dr. Parnell Williams, father of Nicholas Williams."

"And who was *not* at Janet's funeral last year," said Carter.

"What I heard is that they'd had a falling out before the war but now that Parnell is married to the redoubtable Leticia, all is forgotten and forgiven."

"Where'd you hear that?" asked Carter as he slowed down for a red light at Geary.

"I fuck Mr. Webb's chauffeur every now and then."

Carter laughed as he hit the accelerator to move through the intersection. The Chevy made a left leaving a couple of car lengths between Carter's Mercury and Bonnist's Olds.

"When we get up to California, make the left and then get in the left lane. If Bonnist is on his way home, he'll pull into 1814, just past Franklin."

Carter knew most of the houses on that block—the north side, anyway—and was surprised. "You're kidding, right?"

"Nope," said Sam. "Bonnist and his bride live right next door to dear ole daddy who lives at 1828 California with his second wife and almost as many servants as you have."

"I've been there," said Carter as they drove through

the intersection at Pine.

"I figured you had. I remember that fire in '50."

"Well, it wasn't 1828. It was at 1836. That was all wood with no stone masonry and burned down to the ground. It was a total loss."

Sam laughed. "And now we come to the reason why Bonnist works on Folsom Street in the middle of nowhere instead of on the 9th floor of the Newhall Building at California and Battery with his father-in-law at company H.Q."

Carter glanced at Sam. "Yeah. Why isn't he the lead insurance investigator for California Amalgamated?"

"He was until that 1950 fire. He said it wasn't arson but your—"

"Hold on. I investigated that fire with my captain and the chief. That was one of my first big arson investigations."

"Yep," said Sam as Carter followed Bonnist who was making the left onto California right then. "But Bonnist swore to his father-in-law that the Fire Department was wrong."

"But we found evidence that gasoline was used an accelerant. I was the one who found the bottle used for the Molotov cocktail that got the fire started."

"And Bonnist said you were wrong."

"He said I was wrong? Me?"

Sam laughed. "Get in the left lane. Let's watch him park."

"He said I was wrong?"

"No, Carter, he said that the report was wrong. The cops never found whoever did it, right?"

"You'd have to ask Mike since he worked that case at North Station."

"I did and he said it's a cold case." Sam pointed as the Olds pulled into a driveway next to a medium-sized

Victorian house. "There he goes. Dutiful husband back to dutiful wife and their three well-behaved kids. Two boys and a girl." He chuckled. "In the end, Papa Webb fired his son-in-law and that's when Bonnist opened up shop down on Folsom. My, how the mighty have fallen."

"Huh," said Carter as he made a right on Gough, which was the next street past the Bonnist and Webb houses.

"There's a payphone on the southwest corner of Clay and Van Ness."

"I know," said Carter as they drove past Sacramento on the way to Clay. "That's where I'm headed."

"You could tell Nick that you ran into me at Sugar Joe's and that I wanted to talk about Ike."

Carter nodded as he bit the inside of his mouth.

. . .

"Far East Café. May I help you?"

"Hi, I need to talk to one of your patrons, Nick Williams. He's the one who always get the—"

"Yes, sir. Mr. Williams is here. One moment. You wait."

Carter looked over at the Mercury. It was parked on Van Ness and Sam was leaning against the hood, watching the few people who were out and about at 8:15 on a Thanksgiving night.

"Carter? Are you OK?"

"Nick! Sorry I'm just now calling you. About the time Joe and I got done, Sam walked in and asked to talk to me about Ike."

"I called over there and the operator said the line was disconnected."

Not lying, Carter said, "Joe unplugs the phone when

98

he's in a meeting."

"Oh. Well, where are you now?"

"I just left Sam and he reminded me what time it was." Carter frowned to himself. "Any chance I can slide in and join y'all for dinner?"

"Sure. We were late getting here, and they just brought out our food. Should I order your usual? Chop suey?"

"Yes, please. Sorry about this, Nick." Carter felt awful.

"It's OK, Chief. We'll see you in a few."

"Definitely."

. . .

"What a fucking waste of time," muttered Carter once he and Sam were on their way.

"Not really. Now you know who David Bonnist is."

Carter sighed. "Where should I drop you off?"

"You're not driving all the way there, are you? Where are you gonna park on Grant?"

"Oh, right," said Carter. "I'll drop the car off at the house and then I'll take a cable car down or just walk."

"Or get a cab. If you do that, I can take the cab to Ike's place."

Carter nodded.

Chapter 7: Grim news.

1198 Sacramento Street
San Francisco, Cal.
Thursday, November 25, 1954
Half past 8 in the evening

After parking the Mercury in the garage, Carter led Sam up to the kitchen. There, they found Mrs. Strakova playing cards with Mrs. Kopek and Nora.

Sam walked up and asked, "*Tysiqc?*"

Mrs. Kopek nodded and replied in what Carter was pretty sure was Czech since he didn't think Nora spoke Polish.

Sam replied and the three women laughed.

"What kinda game is that?" asked Carter.

"It's like Bridge for three," replied Sam. "Some people call it 'One Thousand' in English."

Carter nodded, watched the ladies play for a moment, and then quietly said, "I need to get to dinner. You coming?"

Before Sam could answer, Carter heard feet

pounding up the stairs that led down to the living quarters below the kitchen. Ferdinand appeared with a grimmer-than-normal expression on his face and said, "Mr. Carter?"

"Can it wait?"

The grimness got even grimmer, if that was possible.

"I don't think it can," said Sam.

"No," added Mrs. Kopek, "it cannot."

Mrs. Strakova threw in her cards. "I will make you dinner, Mr. Carter."

Even if it was just turkey croquettes, Carter knew better than to turn down *that* offer, so he replied, "Thank you," and walked over to the phone.

. . .

"Far East Café. May I help you?" It was the same man as earlier.

"I need to speak to Mr. Williams, again."

"You wait."

Carter looked out the window that looked over the back alley.

Sam suddenly appeared at his elbow and whispered, "I think this might be important. Tell them not to rush home."

Carter nodded.

"Chief?"

"Sorry, Nick. I came home to drop off the car and found a small crisis brewing."

"We're almost done. I'll be there in half an hour or less."

"Nick?"

"Yeah?"

Carter whispered into the phone. "It's a Ferdinand thing. Take your time."

"Oh," was the only thing Nick had to say.

102

"Give us an hour."

"Sure." With that, the line went dead and Carter's heart sank.

. . .

As Mrs. Strakova cooked and Ida chopped, everyone else in the house was seated around the kitchen table. Carter was in his usual spot. Sam was across from him where Nick usually sat. Ferdinand was sitting between Sam and Gustav. Mrs. Kopek was at the end closest to the back door and between Sam and Carter. Nora was on Carter's right.

Mrs. Strakova and Ida were definitely making turkey croquettes, but Carter suspected they would be a lot better than the ones Nick or Carter's mother usually made, not that he had any intention to say that to either of them.

Ferdinand had attempted to talk but was constantly being interrupted by Gustav, Nora, and Ida, all in a mix of English and Czech.

After about five to eight minutes of not being able to follow what Ferdinand was trying to tell him, Carter whistled.

They all turned to stare. All except Ferdinand—he was glaring.

Carter patiently asked, "How about *you*"—he was looking at Ferdinand—"tell Sam all about whatever it is in Czech and *y'all*"—he pointed at Gustav and Nora—"fill in where needed and then *he*"—Carter pointed at Sam—"can translate?"

Gustav nodded. "Yes. Good idea."

Carter looked at Ferdinand. "OK by you?"

With a deep sigh, he replied, "Yes. OK." Turning to Sam, he began to speak in Czech. That went on for about ten minutes, with some additions by Gustav and

103

Nora and some exclamations of dismay coming from Mrs. Strakova and Mrs. Kopek. Carter could tell that, whatever it was, it was going to be upsetting.

Sam, who's face had gotten progressively paler as he listened, finally held up his hand and said something.

Ferdinand nodded and cleared his throat. Gustav leaned against his lover while Nora reached over and patted Ferdinand's hand.

"One moment," said Sam looking at Carter and sounding a lot like Gustav. Sam stood, walked over to the icebox, and pulled out a bottle of Burgie. He removed the cap with his teeth (something that always made Carter shudder in mild horror) and spit it out in his hand. After walking over to the garbage pail to dispose of the cap, he took a long swig. Then he walked back to the table and sat. Looking across at Carter, he said, "This is bad."

"I'm getting that impression."

Sam took another swig of his beer. "You know that Ferdinand is a marathon runner, right?"

Carter nodded.

"Ferdinand went to the games in London in '48 but came in fifth. Then, in '52, he went to Helsinki and took the silver."

"The gold was *Emil Zátopek*," added Gustav with a slight frown. "Also Czech."

"His wife, *Dana Zátopková*, won gold javelin," noted Ida from the counter.

"Anyway," said Sam, "during their training in the spring of '52, there was a man who was regularly coming to the training camp and would deliver propaganda speeches to the men."

"Only men," said Ida, darkly, as she chopped celery.

"Shh!" said Sam.

She stopped to glare at him and then went back to

chopping.

"So, this man spent a lot of time at the training camp. He would inspect the barracks and check on the equipment. That sorta thing." Sam finished his beer. "When they took the train to Helsinki, everyone else traveled third class, but this man had his own compartment."

"Alone," whispered Gustav.

"And, on the trip, he invited some of the male athletes to come into his compartment for special instructions on socialism."

Carter knew exactly what that meant. He doubted anyone was doing much talking at all during all that special instructing. In spite of everything, Carter started grinning.

"Is not funny, Mr. Carter," growled Ferdinand.

Carter cleared his throat. "Of course, not." He looked at Sam. "Go on."

"When they got to the camps outside of Helsinki, this man had his own bungalow."

"Alone," repeated Gustav.

"And he would do the same thing he did on the train."

"Did anyone protest?" asked Carter.

Sam shook his head. "It would've been political suicide."

"So, he was a big deal?"

Sam nodded. "A very big deal."

"Now, he is biggest deal," said Mrs. Kopek.

"But then," said Sam, "he hadn't finished consolidating his power. So, after the Olympics were over, he went back to Prague on the train and that was when his eyes turned to Ferdinand."

Carter glanced over and saw that Gustav had his arms around Ferdinand who was looking at the table. It was one of the saddest things Carter had ever seen.

"So," said Sam, "Ferdinand tried to play along but he was in love with Gustav, and he said as much to this man."

Carter and everyone else jumped when Ferdinand banged the table with his fist.

Sam continued, "And that was when things went from bad to worse. This man had Ferdinand and Gustav committed to the First Faculty Psychiatric Clinic in Prague."

Carter looked at Gustav and asked, "Is that the 'special hospital' you told Nick and me about when you first started working here?"

Gustav nodded.

"So, just like here, then," said Carter, thinking of the horror stories of electro-shock therapy he'd heard about in the last few years.

"No," said Sam, shaking his head. "It's not like here. In Czechoslovakia, they don't do the same kind of thing where they try to cure homosexuals like happens here."

Mrs. Kopek suddenly stood and then quickly made her way downstairs without saying anything.

"Is she OK?" asked Carter, standing up halfway and feeling like he needed to follow her.

Sam replied, "I think she's thinking about Ike."

"I will talk to her later," said Mrs. Strakova from the stove.

Carter nodded and sat back down.

"But, like I was saying," continued Sam, "having Ferdinand and Gustav committed to the psychiatric clinic was out of the ordinary."

"That's good," said Carter with a slight frown. "I guess."

"Well, that was why it was relatively easy for them to

get out once they got married to Ida and Nora."

Ida, who'd finished her chopping, suddenly walked over to Ferdinand and put her arms around his neck from behind. She kissed the top of his head and said something in Czech.

He patted her arm and went from grim to a little less grim.

After Ida went back to the stove to help Mrs. Strakova, Sam said, "So, last spring, these four were able to escape into Austria and, from there, they made it here."

Carter smiled and looked around the table. "And Nick and I are grateful y'all are here."

Nora and Gustav smiled back at him, but Ferdinand was staring at the table.

"So, that brings us to what Sladek from the New York consulate is up to."

Ferdinand banged his hand on the table again.

Sam nodded. "Yesterday, he and Bonnist came by, again, after you and I had left and talked to Gustav and told him what he wants."

Carter looked at Gustav, whose eyes were welling up with tears. "Which is what?"

"He wants them to go back to Prague."

"But they're not going to, right?"

"Did you know they all have family back in Prague?"

"And *Plzeň*," added Ida from the sink.

"Oh," said Carter as he sat back, feeling his hands getting clammy. "Are they in trouble?"

"Not yet," replied Sam.

"But soon," said Gustav.

Carter sighed. "Why does he want them to go back? And is it just Gustav and Ferdinand?"

"It is me," replied Ferdinand. "Only."

Gustav leaned over, kissed his lover on the cheek,

and whispered something in Czech.

"That man we were talking about earlier?" said Sam.

"The one who's now a big deal, but wasn't then?"

Sam chuckled. "Yeah. Him. He's going to be in New York next week at the U.N. and wants Ferdinand to fly back to Prague with him when he goes home."

Without even thinking about it, Carter shook his head. "No. Not gonna happen."

Sam pressed his lips together. "But here's the rub..." He looked over at Gustav who was frowning.

"What?" asked Carter.

Jesus! What else could there be?

Studying the table, Sam said, "Bonnist knows what happens here last year." He looked up. "When Nick's father..." He raised his eyebrows. "And when Mike...." He bit his lip. "You know... right before the funeral."

"Damn," said Carter as he put his hand over his eyes.

. . .

Back in May of 1953, Nick's younger sister, Janet, had died in what the police first thought was an accident. She was driving down Broadway, heading towards the tunnel, and, according to witnesses, had sped up. She'd veered all over the road, honking, and ended up crashing into a brick wall. Everyone who saw it claimed that she'd intentionally crashed the car where she had in order to avoid hitting anyone else. She died that night in the hospital. Nick and Carter were by her bedside when she did.

Nick then tracked down the actual killer, a mechanic by the name of Marty, who'd worked for McAlister Buick. He'd tampered with the transmission of Janet's car. He'd done that when she'd brought it in to be serviced. He'd recognized her name and the fact that she was Dr. Williams's daughter. He'd also suspected she would be loaded and that there would be money at her house out by the Presidio.

He'd known about Dr. Williams, Janet, and the house out by the Presidio because of his lover, Marlene. She was working for Dr. Williams as one of a long line of assistants he'd had over the years. He'd actually fallen in love with her and, before she and her lover killed Janet, was planning on proposing.

The whole mess had come to a head, here, in the office. Nick had figured out what was going on, had gone to the North Station to grab Mike, and the two had raced over to Sacramento Street. Once they'd arrived, they'd found Dr. Williams in a stand-off with Marty and Marlene who were demanding he open the safe in the office floor and give them all the cash he had. Dr. Williams was, naturally, refusing to do so and even claiming there was no cash to be had (Nick later told Carter there was probably around two million stashed in the floor safe).

Although Nick was standing by the front door and didn't see it happen, Dr. Williams shot Marty dead and Mike saw him do it.

Carter had never read the report, but he knew that Mike had arranged with his captain to cover things up so that Dr. Williams wouldn't get in trouble. In the end, Marlene was sent down to the California women's prison in Chino, outside of Los Angeles, after confessing to her role in the plot. As far as Carter knew, she was still serving time there.

. . .

Even though Mrs. Strakova was just about to fry up the croquettes, Carter stood and said to Sam, "We need to talk by ourselves for a moment."

He nodded and followed Carter out into the dining

room and through to the office. Once there, Carter closed the door and blocked it with his body in case anyone else tried to follow them inside. He doubted they would, but he wanted to be doubly cautious.

"Back to the scene of the crime?" asked Sam with a grin as he leaned against the trophy case.

Carter felt his hand go up to his chin again. With a tremendous amount of will power, he forced himself to relax and to breathe.

Try not to kill your employees!

Sam looked abashed. "Sorry, Carter. Bad timing."

"How much do any of them in the kitchen know about what happened here that day?"

"Ferdinand said he didn't understand what Sladek was talking about. All Sladek told them was that they knew about what happened here in May of '53."

Carter took a couple of deep breaths. "How do *you* know?"

Sam slowly shrugged. "I just happen to know."

"Did Mike tell you?"

Sam snorted. "Big Boss? Are you kidding me? Really?"

"How'd you find out, Sam?"

He shrugged again. "I just hear things."

Carter sighed. "Tell me exactly what you know."

Sam looked over, seemed to consider it, and then shook his head. "Nah."

Stepping forward, Carter hissed, "Tell me."

"Fine." Sam crossed his arms. "I know from a source in the police department that Mike paid off his captain to falsify the report and to say that Mike wasn't in here when the gun went off."

Carter tried as hard as he could not to betray any emotion.

Mike paid off his captain? With what money? Mike didn't

have a thousand bucks to his name, if that much, before Nick hired him to run Consolidated Security.

"The story is that Mike told Nick to leave before his captain arrived. Once the captain got there, the gal who was in on it was already in handcuffs. Apparently, the captain convinced her to agree to Mike's version of the story. Then he—the captain, that is—he went to the D.A. and pressed him to only give her three years down in Chino." Sam blinked. "You didn't know any of this, did you?"

"Of course, I did," replied Carter as calmly as he could.

"No, you didn't. I can see it in your face. You're just as surprised now as you were in the kitchen when I told you what Sladek told Ferdinand." Sam was grinning right then.

Carter had a sudden awakening to an idea that came out of nowhere. Sam was like a vacuum. He went all over the City and sucked up tidbits of information. And he stored them until he could use them. Carter had an awful feeling that the fact that Sam knew all the dirty details about that day in May of 1953 was almost as dangerous as the fact that Sladek and Bonnist knew. Maybe even more dangerous...

Sam sniffed the air. "I'm hungry. Let's go eat."

Putting out his arm to block the other man, Carter said, "What do we do now?"

"We eat and then you need to bring Nick in on this and do it tonight."

That surprised Carter. "What made you change your mind?"

Sam's eyes widened. "This is now an international affair. You, me, and Walter can't handle this on our own. We need everyone at the office to get together and figure out how to take care of this."

"But you don't say anything about the blackmail Sladek has on Mike and Dr. Williams. Got that?"

Sam nodded. "Sure. You'll have to tell Nick, though. And Mike." He then grinned. "Better you than me."

"That makes sense," said Carter, mostly to himself.

"And with that," said Sam, "I think I'll skip dinner. I've got a hot date, so I'll leave by the front door." He pushed past Carter and was gone before either could say goodbye.

. . .

Back in the kitchen, the croquettes were still frying on the stove, but looking golden brown. Carter said, "Sam had to leave," as he walked over to the icebox and got out a bottle of Burgie for himself. "Anyone else want a beer?" he asked.

No one answered, but suddenly Ferdinand was standing next to him. "Mr. Carter. We talk."

With a nod, Carter said, "Sure. Let me—"

"Now," said Ferdinand, getting very close and looking mildly threatening.

"OK," said Carter, putting his bottle back in the icebox with a sigh.

Ferdinand stomped out into the dining room and Carter followed him. They ended up out in the garden, in the dark and in the cold. Carter was about to shut the door when Gustav suddenly showed up with a frown on his face.

Once they were all outside and the door was closed, Carter turned to Ferdinand and asked, "Are you OK?"

"No. I am no OK."

"He is very angry," offered Gustav.

"I can see that."

112

With a long finger, Ferdinand poked Carter in the chest. "I go *Praha*. You no tell Mr. Nick."

Carter grabbed the man's finger. "Don't poke at me."

Ferdinand pulled his hand away while Gustav started crying and mumbling in Czech. Ferdinand crossed his arms and just shook his head.

"English!" said Carter with more than a little impatience in his voice.

"He can no go!" wailed Gustav. "I will go if he go."

"No!" barked Ferdinand. Pointing at Gustav, he said, "He stay. He find other love. Mr. Nick must no know." He leaned towards Carter. "Understand, you? He no know!"

Why not just give Ferdinand a gun? Then he could kill Sladek, Bonnist, and whoever this Czech big-wig was who had the hots for him. That would solve a myriad of problems.

But Carter was against violence and murder and he knew things like that never solved any problem. They could all end up going to jail. No one—not the police, not the F.B.I., not any part of the government—no one in authority would help them. Quite the opposite, as a matter of fact. This was just the thing someone like J. Edgar Hoover would love to find out about. He could use it to get rid of Nick and Carter and the whole Consolidated Security team full of homosexuals of all stripes. And nothing would make the director of the F.B.I. happier than that.

Sam was right. They needed Nick and Mike and everyone at the office in on this problem. This was too big to manage without more help. And they had plenty of resources at the office to draw from. In fact, there were—

"No tell Mr. Nick!" yelled Ferdinand one more time, just for good measure.

"Look," said Carter with a placating smile, "I'm

hungry and I'm gonna go eat. No one is gonna tell anyone anything until tomorrow." Sam had said he should talk to Nick before going to bed. Carter knew himself well enough to know that he'd be more clear-headed after a good night's sleep. Maybe an option he hadn't thought of yet would come to him in the light of morning... Surely, the whole thing could wait one more night...

Chapter 8: Fireside musing.

1198 Sacramento Street
San Francisco, Cal.
Thursday, November 25, 1954
Close to midnight

Nick was pouting on the Chesterfield.

"Come to bed, son," urged Carter.

"Why won't you tell me what this is all about?"

"It's personal and we need to give Ferdinand room to breathe. They're all confined downstairs in that little space. The least we can do is give him his privacy when he asks for it."

Nick sighed. "I guess you're right. I just feel like you're keeping something from me."

Carter was tempted to tell Nick the whole thing right then and there.

I'll have a clearer mind in the morning.

And he was right. A good night's sleep would make it easier to tell Nick and Mike everything when they got to the office.

Nick turned to look over at the bed. "What are you keeping from me, Chief?"

"It's just what I told you. Ferdinand talked to me in confidence." None of that was a lie.

Nick stared at him for a long moment and then finally stood and walked over to the bed. He leaned against the bedpost and broke into a grin. "Does this qualify as a fight?"

Carter grinned back. "If we get to have make-up sex, then, hell, yeah, it does."

. . .

An hour later, it was finally over. Usually, Carter never had any trouble doing for Nick what Nick wanted done, but on that night...

Things had gotten easier when Carter had told himself that the point was to make Nick happy. As soon as that thought formed in his mind, suddenly everything shifted into gear and the train started steaming down the track.

Carter leaned over and kissed Nick on the back of his neck. "G'night, Boss."

Nick replied, "Mmm," and then was out.

Carter carefully slid off the bed and walked over to the fire where he sat down on the floor and crossed his legs. The blaze on the hearth was about halfway through its natural life, so there was nothing to do other than to maybe move some of the embers around a little. Which Carter did with the poker.

As he gazed into the dancing flames, he thought about the waves he'd seen down around Carmel. The ocean and a fire had a lot in common. As much as you might think you could predict what each would do, you would more than likely be wrong. Carter loved that about waves and flames. They danced and bobbed and weaved around like the most skillful boxer you could imagine. You never knew where the next one would go —a flame, a wave, or a fist.

Thinking of fists reminded Carter of Ferdinand.

Why doesn't he want me to say anything to Nick? Does he know what it would do to Consolidated Security and all their lives if anyone found out about Mike filing a false report?

That couldn't be it. Sam had said Ferdinand didn't know much about any of that.

Then why? What was Ferdinand doing?

Carter watched the flames dance and bob and weave for a long while. He thought about how intertwined their lives—his and Nick's—had quickly become with so many people.

In the months and years before Janet had been murdered, he and Nick had lived rather quiet lives. The biggest thing they'd ever done up to that point was to buy the house on Hartford and take a cross-country trip to New York City to see *South Pacific*.

Then, after Janet had died and he, Mike, Carlo, and Ben had all been fired, they'd started up Consolidated Security. Or, rather, Nick had the idea and wisely handed it off to Mike. Since then, their circle of friends, acquaintances, and business associates had exploded.

They'd moved into Nick's grandfather's house and that was how Czechoslovakia, a country thousands of miles away, had become part of their lives.

Nick had solved a number of tricky cases in the 18 months since Janet had died. One of those involved the death of Carter's own father back in Albany. Nick had figured out who really killed the old son-of-a-bitch. So, instead of a colored man being railroaded by the local sheriff, the white man who'd done the deed because he'd lost his inheritance over a poker game had been convicted of the murder and was sent to the electric chair at the end of 1953.

As Carter sat in front of the fire, watching the flames jump and move, he started to get drowsy. He thought about getting up and going to bed, but he wasn't ready. Not yet.

He needed to figure out what was going on with Ferdinand.

Why didn't he want Nick to know? Who was the man in Czechoslovakia who wanted Ferdinand back? Why hadn't he asked Sam to tell him the name? Why was he such a big deal?

As his eyes closed, Carter resolved to talk to Sam before going to Nick and Mike. After all, he needed all the facts before he presented his case...

. . .

"Order!" boomed the frowning judge from his bench as he banged his gavel.

Carter looked around the courtroom. It was like being in a movie. He was standing in what the English called "the dock." His hands were tied in front of him, and he was leaning against a railing.

The room was empty except for two men. One was the judge, who was wearing black robes and an old-fashioned white wig and was frowning at Carter.

Although he could hear people whispering behind him, the only other person he could see was the prosecutor. That man, who was not wearing a wig, had his back to Carter as he looked at a big pile of notes and books and papers on a wide table.

After what seemed like an eternity, the judge said, "Does the crown wish to proceed?"

"Yes, my lord," replied the prosecutor. His accent

wasn't English, though. It was Southern. Georgian, to be specific.

"Proceed."

"My lord, what we have here is the simple case of a liar!" The prosecutor turned and pointed at Carter who gasped. It was his own father!

"This man," said his father as he pointed, "who goes by the name of Carter Woodrow Wilson Jones, is being held by the crown in the matter of Williams versus Jones. Soon, my lord, I will bring the complainant, one Nicholas Williams, into the courtroom and my lord will hear his testimony as to the many lies spoken by Jones, the defendant." As he spoke, Carter's father was strutting around the courtroom like he was William Jennings Bryant in the Scopes "Monkey" Trial.

"But I'm doing it because I'm trying to protect Nick!" exclaimed Carter.

"Protect him?" asked his father in an accusatory voice. "Why?"

Carter thought for a moment. "I don't know."

"You don't know?" asked the judge from the bench.

"No, sir, I don't. All I know is that I love Nick and I want him to be safe."

The judge seemed to consider that. He nodded for a moment and then looked at Carter's father. "Mr. Prosecutor?"

"Yes, my lord?"

"This court will continue this trial. It seems not all the evidence is at hand."

"But my lord!" roared Carter's father. "This is unfair! I am ready to bring Nicholas Williams out to testify." He turned to look up at Carter. "And then you'll be in trouble, boy. A world of trouble."

Carter leaned back. He felt the wall behind him as he cowered in the bottom of the wardrobe. His father was towering over him and had a belt in his hand. "What did I say about you and Bobby playin' with them nigger kids?"

Carter couldn't speak.

"Get out here, boy, and take your medicine."

Carter shook his head.

His father reached in and grabbed him by the arm and—

. . .

"Wake up!"

Opening his eyes, Carter could see that Nick was standing over him with a worried expression on his face.

"You were having a bad dream."

"I was?" As Carter sat up, all the details of the dream he'd just had came flooding in.

"Was it about your father again?"

Carter nodded as he stood.

"Come back to bed," said Nick. He took Carter by the hand and led him over.

"Nick."

"Yeah?"

"There's something I need to tell you."

Nick pushed him towards the bed. "Get in first, then we can talk. I'm cold."

Carter followed instructions and got in. Nick did the same and pulled Carter towards him. Resting his head on Nick's furry belly, Carter said, "It's about Ferdinand."

Nick ran his hand through Carter's hair. "Hush. You were right. It's none of my business. If Ferdinand wants me to know about whatever's going on, he'll tell me."

Nick rubbed Carter's arm. "I'm just sorry you're in the middle of it."

"You are?"

"I am glad, though, that he has a friend like you that he can talk to."

Carter didn't know what to say to that, so he just nodded.

Chapter 9: Introducing the First Secretary.

1198 Sacramento Street
San Francisco, Cal.
Friday, November 26, 1954
Just past dawn

Carter turned over and reached out for Nick but found an empty spot where his husband should have been.

He opened his eyes and looked around. The sun was up and there was no fog blocking the blue sky, which was nice. The bathroom door was open, and the light was off. That meant Nick was not taking a shower or doing anything else.

Carter propped himself up on his elbow and yawned. By the smell of things, breakfast was underway downstairs and, apparently, Nick was down there as well.

He was about to get up and get dressed when he

heard a knock on the bedroom door. "Come in."

The door pushed open, and Ferdinand looked in. "Mr. Carter?"

"Come in."

Ferdinand walked in, closed the door, and stood by the side of the bed.

"Good morning."

"Yes," replied Ferdinand with the slightest grin, which was his version of a smile.

"What's up?"

The grin vanished. "I apologize."

"For what?" asked Carter as he sat up.

"Last night."

"You don't need to apologize, Ferdinand. I can't imagine how all of this must feel to you."

"Is bad."

"I haven't told Nick anything although he knows you and I talked and that you were upset."

"Thank you, Mr. Carter."

"Do you mind if I ask you a question about all this?"

"Yes?"

"What is the name of the man in Czechoslovakia who did this to you?"

Ferdinand's unsmiling face went hard. "*Antonín Novotný*. He is First Secretary."

"First Secretary? Of the Communist Party?"

"Yes."

Carter nodded. "Is that like what Stalin was? Does that mean he runs the country?"

"Yes."

"Wow."

"Yes."

The doorbell rang right then.

"Who could that be?" asked Carter. He looked at his watch. It was half past 7.

"I go," replied Ferdinand before turning, walking out of the bedroom, and closing the door behind him.

. . .

Carter was pulling a green sweater over his head when he heard a knock on the door followed by Gustav saying, "Mr. Carter?"

"Come in."

Gustav opened the door and walked into the room. "There is problem."

As he straightened his sweater, Carter asked, "What kind of a problem?"

"*Alexander Sladek* is here. He wish talk to Mr. Nick."

"Did he bring David Bonnist with him? The American guy?"

"Yes."

"Where are they?"

"In office."

Considering what Sam had told him, that was just about the worst place to put them. But Gustav had no way of knowing that and Carter couldn't think of a better option.

"What did you tell them about Nick?"

"That he is at office."

"And where is Nick?"

"Ferdinand take him to garage to talk about problem with Buick."

"What problem?"

Gustav grinned a little. "There is no problem."

Carter walked over and kissed Gustav on the forehead. "Good man."

. . .

125

Opening the door with a flourish, Carter opted for the dramatic and said, "Good morning, gentlemen. What can I do for you?"

Sladek was standing by the trophy case and inspecting the airplanes. Bonnist was bent over and looking at the Chinese table in the middle of the room, which was hiding the safe in the floor.

When Dr. Williams had killed Marty back in 1953, that spot had been covered by a Persian rug. Now there was an octagonal table, designed and constructed by a man in Chinatown. It contained an ingenious built-in mechanism that would cause the table to slide over to the side and reveal the safe. It would only move if you tripped a hidden lever. As far as Carter knew, Nick and his father were the only two who could find the lever. Not even Carter knew how to swing the table to the side. Even then, you had to have the combination to the safe and Nick was the only one with that.

Sladek pointed to the glass. "These are the hallmarks of a decadent bourgeois attitude regarding the oppression of the workers."

Carter ignored that just like he'd ignored similar comments from Ferdinand and Ida when they'd first arrived. Instead, he said, "I don't remember catching your name when you paid us a visit on Wednesday morning." Remembering that Bonnist had talked to him on the phone just the day before, Carter kept his Southern accent at bay and tried to sound more like Nick using his high-hat voice and less like Howard T. Albertson.

The Czechoslovakian looked at him in the eye. "My name is *Alexander Sladek* and I have come here for *Ferdinand Zak*. He is needed back in his homeland."

"Why?"

"He was being trained for the party leadership and

his skills are required as we continue the implementation of socialism in Czechoslovakia."

Carter tilted his head. "You didn't seem to think he was party material when you threw him in the psychiatric clinic in Prague."

Bonnist, who had been ignoring Carter and Sladek and had remained bent over and focused on the table, suddenly stopped and stood up.

"Errors have been made along the way since the Red Army liberated our country from German oppression. The party is prepared to offer *Zak* a prominent position with all the attributes accorded to his rank, as a sign of goodwill."

Carter crossed his arms. "I understand you tried to convince him to return on Wednesday when the two of you stopped by a second time and he refused."

"Further education of *Zak* may be required," said Sladek in an ominous voice.

"Well, this is America, bub, and he is free to come or go as he pleases."

Sladek smiled a little. It was as frightening as Ferdinand's smile. "But what of his family? And that of *Gustav Bilek*? And others? They are in Prague and the party has taken a keen interest in their activities and their, shall we say, *welfare*."

Carter didn't smile because it wasn't really funny, but Sladek was sounding more and more like a Nazi right out of a movie like *Casablanca* or *Above Suspicion*.

Bonnist suddenly said, "Let's cut to the chase." He looked over at Carter. "I know what happened here on May 15th of 1953 and, unless you want it splashed all over the front page of the *Examiner*, you'll convince Ferdinand Zak to go back with Mr. Sladek when he leaves for New York on Sunday."

Wondering what, exactly, Bonnist knew, Carter played dumb and frowned. "May the 15th? Here?" He looked at Sladek and then back at Bonnist. "That was before I moved in here. I have no idea what you're talking about."

Bonnist raised an eyebrow. "Is that so, Mr. Jones? Would it surprise you to know that Dr. Parnell Williams shot and murdered one Martin Cox? Mr. Cox did not commit suicide as was noted in the official incident report filed by Lieutenant Michael Robertson of the North Station of the San Francisco Police Department. Lieutenant Robertson was at the scene in this very room when the murder occurred, and he lied about what happened."

Carter deepened his frown as he realized he'd never heard Marty's full name before. Nor did he know that the death had been reported as suicide.

Bonnist walked over to Carter's desk and picked up an ivory letter opener. As Bonnist examined the thing, he continued, "It would be unfortunate if Mr. Robertson were to be called to testify before the grand jury." He looked up at Carter. "And what about Dr. Williams? He'll be put on trial for murder. From what I've heard, it was not self-defense. It was cold-blooded murder." Bonnist smiled a little and then tossed the letter opener onto the desk. "What do you think about that?"

"I think you must be lying. Dr. Williams never shot anyone, and Mike always played it straight when he was on the force."

Bonnist chuckled. "'Played it straight'? Hardly. He was about as straight as a feather boa on a camel's back."

Carter blinked at that phrase. He got the feather boa part, but what did a camel's back have to do with being a homosexual?

"But you know that. You employ more homosexuals than anyone outside of Hollywood or Broadway."

"Mr. Jones," said Sladek, looking a little uncomfortable with the turn the conversation had taken, "the party's proposition is clear. *Zak* will return to Prague and take his rightful place as a rising—"

With sudden insight, Carter interrupted the man. "He's just as much of a homosexual as me or Mike Robertson."

Sladek began to turn red.

Carter knew he was on the right track, so he stepped towards the man who was only about 5'7" or so, at the most. That meant Carter had a good seven inches on him and intended to use it to his advantage. With a grin, he said, "And that's why you want Ferdinand back, isn't it?"

Backing up, Sladek put out his hand. "I am no pervert."

"Really?" asked Carter, turning his grin into a smile while he looked the man up and down as if he was a tasty morsel. "That's not what I heard. I heard that Ferdinand was wanted back in Prague because the First Secretary misses his handsome and virile plaything." Carter was standing right over the man who was backed against the wall. He reached down and tapped Sladek on the tip of his nose. "You're just about as cute as a button." That was a blatant lie. The man had a pasty white face and no charisma to speak of. But it had the intended effect. Sladek was beginning to squirm. "Maybe you and me should get more acquainted. Waddaya say?"

Before Sladek could reply, Carter felt something crack, hard, against his back and then break when it hit the floor. He whipped around and saw the remnants of a large vase that usually sat in the corner. Kicking the shards out of the way, Carter reached out, grabbed Bonnist by the tie, and yanked him closer by a foot or so. "What the hell was that?"

"Leave me alone, you fuckin' pansy!" yelled Bonnist.

"Pansy?" asked Carter, remembering the last time someone had called him that which was, coincidentally, over at Grace Cathedral and on the 16th of May in 1953. It was during Janet's funeral and it was Dr. Williams who'd used that very word.

"Yeah," replied Bonnist, trying to sound tougher than he looked. The poor guy was a pencil-pusher. He was supposed to be an insurance investigator, not a private dick. He didn't have the chops to play dirty pool, even though he'd given it his best shot with the vase.

Carter pushed Bonnist back, aiming for the Chinese table. And he made his target. Bonnist hit it with his ass and then flipped over onto the floor where he began to moan in pain. Carter doubted he'd broken the guy's back, but he figured things down there would be sore for a while.

"Get up," he barked, kicking one of Bonnist's legs with the toe of his shoe. He didn't kick hard. He just wanted Bonnist to take the hint.

"I can't," moaned the guy.

"What's wrong?" asked Carter as a frightened Gustav opened the door. When he saw what was going on, he began to laugh.

Behind Carter, Sladek began to yell in Czech.

Mrs. Kopek arrived right then with Nora on her heels.

"Is he OK?" asked the older woman.

Carter bent over, put his hands under Bonnist's arms, and lifted him to his feet. After letting go, Carter declared, "He'll live."

Bonnist stumbled to the door. When he got there, he leaned against the wall and said, "You'll regret this, Jones. The whole lousy story is gonna be on the front page of the *Examiner*. Mark my words." With that he somehow made it to the front door.

Sladek walked around the broken shards of the vase, stopped in front of Gustav, and began to berate him in Czech. When Gustav spit in the man's face, Sladek raised his hand and slapped the kid, and hard.

Carter took two giant steps forward and grabbed Sladek by the collar. He lifted the man off the floor and carried him to the front door, which was open following Bonnist's departure, and dropped him on the front porch like a piece of lead. Carter slammed the door closed, locked it, and then turned to Gustav. "You OK?"

With a nod, the kid walked up to Carter, put his arms around him, and squeezed hard. "Thank you, Mr. Carter."

Patting Gustav on the back of the head, Carter said, "You're welcome. Where's Nick?"

Into Carter's sweater, Gustav said, "Ferdinand say to take drive in Buick down to McAlister on Van Ness. They go together. For to be safe."

Carter leaned back and kissed Gustav on the forehead again. "Good man."

Chapter 10: A breakfast meeting.

Ruby's Grille
Corner of Mission and 5th
San Francisco, Cal.
Friday, November 26, 1954
Later that morning

Carter looked up from his coffee as Sam and Walter both walked in the diner. Sam waved at a waitress who was handing out plates of food and got a smile in reply. She was the same waitress who'd brought Carter his coffee.

Walter slid in across from Carter and Sam joined him on the outside.

"Where's Nick?" asked Sam.

"He's with Ferdinand at McAlister Buick."

Sam looked at his watch. "This early?"

Carter nodded. "Nick called from the dealership right after I talked to you. He said Ferdinand is worried about the transmission slipping and the brakes needing to be replaced too often. Ferdinand made them call in old man McAllister, himself."

"Brakes?" squeaked Walter. "This is San Francisco." He pushed up his glasses with his finger. "I always say that everyone who lives here should have theirs changed every three thousand miles."

Carter grinned. "I'm sure poor Mr. McAlister is saying something like that right about now."

Their waitress walked up right then. "Hiya, Sam. Long time, no see. What can I getcha?"

"Hi, Julie. I'll take some coffee." He looked at Walter.

"Do you have fresh orange juice?"

"Sure, hon." She grinned. "This is California, right?"

"I'll take that, please."

"One coffee and one fresh-squeezed. Any grub for any of you fellas?" She pulled out her pad and a pencil.

Sam shook his head. "I already ate."

Carter looked over at Walter. "I'm going to order something. You want anything?"

He nodded. "May I have a bowl of oatmeal, no raisins, and a fruit salad?"

Julie started writing. "Oatmeal, hold the raisins." She looked over at Walter. "Just so youse know, the only fruit we got that ain't from a can are oranges and grapefruits."

"Thanks. I'll take half a grapefruit, then."

"You want that little cherry?"

"No, ma'am."

She smiled at that and then looked at Carter. "What about you, Red?"

"Three eggs scrambled, a double order of chewy bacon, hashed-brown potatoes, and wheat toast."

She nodded as she finished her scribbling. "Got it. Be right back with coffee and the fresh-squeezed."

After she walked away, Sam said, "So, tell us what

happened." He glanced at Walter. "I already told him about the big reveal last night."

Carter nodded and then quickly told the two of them all the details of his conversation with Bonnist and Sladek. While he was talking, Julie dropped off Sam's coffee and Walter's orange juice. Carter finished his story with an account of how he'd dumped Sladek on the front porch of the house and then locked the door.

Sam looked impressed. "I wish I coulda seen Bonnist trying to break your back with that vase."

Walter giggled at that.

"It isn't really funny," said Carter, unable to keep himself from smiling.

Sam covered his mouth, shook his head, and elbowed Walter. "It's not funny at all."

To Carter's delight and surprise, Walter looked at Sam and then at Carter before exclaiming, "Are you serious? It's better than a Looney Tunes cartoon!"

The three men all laughed.

"Seriously, though," said Carter, looking at Walter and then Sam. "What do we do?"

"Well, as soon as we finish eating," replied Sam, "we call Mike and have him meet us at the office."

Walter nodded. "Yes. Even though the office is closed, that's what we should do."

"Closed?" asked Carter before remembering they'd decided to make extend the Thanksgiving holiday and make it a four-day weekend. "Oh, right." He pressed his lips together. "But there's a problem with that."

"What?" asked Sam.

"The reason Nick is at McAlister's isn't because there's a problem with the car."

"Oh?"

"It's because Ferdinand made it clear to me last night

that he does not want Nick to know about any of this. When Sladek and Bonnist showed up, Ferdinand took Nick down to the garage on the pretense that something was wrong with the car."

"Why doesn't he want Mr. Williams to know?" asked Walter.

Carter shrugged. "I have no idea. But Ferdinand even threatened to go back to Prague."

"Wow," said Walter as Sam began to stir his coffee even though he hadn't put any sugar in it.

"We have a couple of days to figure this out," continued Carter. "If Ferdinand doesn't go back to New York with Sladek, then Bonnist will leak the story about Mike and Dr. Williams to the *Examiner* for Monday's edition." He smiled a little at Walter who was staring at him through his glasses, looking just like an owl. "I think that, between the three of us, we can figure something out by Saturday night." Carter looked at Sam who was still stirring his coffee. "Don't you think so?"

Sam started to shake his head.

"What?" asked Carter.

Exhaling, Sam slid down a little in his seat. "Sometimes, I wish I really understood what the Germans did to those kids."

Julie arrived right then with plates and bowls of food. Once those were passed out and Carter's coffee had been topped off, she walked over to take care of a couple with a teenaged son who'd just walked in. To Carter's eyes, the son looked like he was angry about something. Carter knew that, at his age, it could be literally anything. That thought brought him back to what Sam had said about the Germans. As he picked up a slice of bacon, Carter asked, "What did you mean by what you said earlier about the Germans?"

Sam reached over and took one of Carter's slices of

bacon and ate half of it before replying. "For the life of me, I cannot imagine why they don't want Nick to know. But, having spent some time with all four of them and talking to Anna about it, I've begun to realize that living under the occupation as teenagers really screwed them all up."

"Of course," said Walter as he blew on his spoon of steaming oatmeal. "That must have been an awful thing to go through."

Carter nodded. "It must have, but what does that have to do with them not wanting Nick to know?"

Sam shrugged. "Beats me." He finished the other half of the stolen slice of bacon. "But Ferdinand was serious, huh?"

"As a heart attack," replied Carter. "*Deadly* serious might be another way to describe it."

Walter sighed a little. "But he's so handsome, though."

Carter and Sam both grinned a little.

"Gotta crush?" asked Sam.

Looking around the table, Walter replied, "Who doesn't?"

Carter raised his hand a little. "Me."

With a laugh, Sam said, "That's because you lift weights with him and get in the ring. That's always killed all of my crushes. Once I see a man's fist headed my way, my dick goes limp."

Carter and Walter both laughed.

"I *beg* your pardon!" exclaimed a woman's voice behind Carter's head.

Sam leaned over and said, "Sorry about that, lady. Gym talk."

"I'm *sure*," was her frosty reply.

"Look," said Sam, turning serious. "The point isn't *why* Ferdinand wants to keep this a secret from Nick.

137

The point is that it puts us in a bind."

Carter nodded.

"But does it?" quietly asked Walter, as he looked up at the ceiling with a spoonful of oatmeal in his hand.

"What do you mean?" asked Carter.

Walter swallowed his oatmeal with a frown. Then he took another spoonful and also swallowed it.

"Walter?"

"Shh," whispered Sam. Leaning over the table, he glanced at Walter and added, "The *big brain* is working. Can't you see the red and green lights and hear the beeps and boops?"

Carter chuckled and ate some of his eggs.

After about a minute of Walter meditatively slurping down his oatmeal, he finally said, "Well, if nothing else, we can buy some time."

"How?" asked Sam.

Walter looked at Carter. "I can get in touch with Mr. Bonnist and tell him I work for the *Examiner*. I know one of the reporters there and he's told me all about how they use sources and the like."

Sam stroked his chin and nodded thoughtfully. "Yeah. You could call him and tell him you heard around town that he's got something big on that snooty Dr. Williams."

"Has he seen you?" asked Carter.

"No," replied Walter. "But I was planning on phoning him."

Sam got a big smile on his face. "The office is empty today, right?"

Walter nodded.

Looking at Carter, Sam said, "How's your typing, Red?"

Chapter 11: We have our sources.

Offices of Consolidated Security, Inc.
777 Bush Street
San Francisco, Cal.
Friday, November 26, 1954
Half past 10 in the morning

Carter was sitting at Marnie's desk, with her Olympia typewriter right in front of him, and was typing on it as well as he was able to. After digging through her files, he'd found an old report from 1951 about a job Nick had done for Pacific Gas & Electric. While Walter was on the phone, Carter sat at the typewriter and re-typed Nick's report. The idea was to make it sound like Walter was calling from inside the *Examiner's* newsroom.

Walter was talking with Bonnist on Robert's phone. Even as Carter was typing, he was holding Marnie's phone in the crook of his neck. Sam had opened up the mouthpiece end of the receiver and removed the mic so that Carter wouldn't have to worry about making noise while listening in on the call. Sam had also done the same thing with Nick's phone so he could listen in on the call as well.

The line was ringing. Sam had suggested they call the home number first. After taking the beating Carter had given him earlier, Sam doubted that Bonnist had gone into the office.

"Hello?" It was a woman's voice.

"Yes, hello, there," said Walter in an efficient voice. "Is Mr. Bonnist available?"

"May I say who's calling?"

"This is Walter Marcello with the *San Francisco Examiner*." Walter had said he would use his real name. The *Examiner* was famous for not using bylines, so it didn't really matter. "I'm a reporter."

"A *reporter*?" The woman sounded shocked.

"Yes. You see, uh, I have a few questions to ask Mr. Bonnist. You can tell him, if you like, that it's in regards to the Williams and Robertson matter."

"Beg pardon? The *what* matter?"

"Williams and Robertson."

"Well, lemme see if he wants to come to the phone. He had a slight fender bender this mornin' and has taken to his bed."

"Thank you."

Carter heard a clunking sound as the phone was placed on a table. He could hear someone walking away. He stopped typing and looked over at Walter who mouthed, "This might take a while." Carter nodded.

But it didn't take a while at all. Within a few seconds, Carter heard another phone pick up and Bonnist say, "Hello? This is David Bonnist. Who's speaking?"

"Hello, Mr. Bonnist. This is Walter Marcello from the *Examiner*. I was wondering if I could ask you a few questions about a story I'm working on for the Sunday edition. It's in regards to Parnell Williams and Michael Robertson."

"*How* the hell did you hear about *that*?"

"I work for the *Examiner*, Mr. Bonnist," replied Walter in a smug tone of voice. "We have our sources."

"I bet it's one of the ten people who work for that queer, Nick Williams, on Nob Hill."

"I really can't say. But I was wondering if you could confirm some of what I've heard and, maybe, give me anything else you might know about the matter. I can keep you anonymous or I can mention you by name. My editor has agreed to either proposition."

"How much?"

"Provided my editor approves my story, I'm authorized to pay fifty in cash and send it out today by messenger."

"Lowell Wilson pays seventy-five when I give him stories on the mayor."

"That's the City Hall beat, Mr. Bonnist. My purview is a little different."

"But this is the story of the year."

"True. I can mention Mr. Wilson to my editor when I submit my story. He'll probably authorize seventy-five."

"I want a hundred for something this juicy."

"Let's don't get greedy, Mr. Bonnist."

"One more thing before I give you what I know. This story has to wait for Monday. One of *my* sources needs that to happen. I wasn't even planning on calling Lowell until Sunday morning after the paper was on the streets."

"I don't think that will be a problem. To tell you the truth, a Monday story will be better for me."

"I bet." Bonnist sniffed into the phone. "Where do we begin?"

"How about I tell you what I know and then you tell

me what I'm missing?"

"Sure. Go right ahead."

"From what I know, it appears that, on Friday, May 15th of 1953, when Martin 'Marty' Cox died in the home of Dr. Parnell Williams at 1198 Sacramento, he did not commit suicide as the police incident report indicated. Apparently, Mr. Cox was shot by Dr. Williams in cold blood. Further, Lieutenant Michael Robertson saw the shooting take place and falsified the report. Lieutenant Robertson, of course, was fired by the mayor that very night after being exposed as a pervert and is now the president of something called Consolidated Security. Am I correct so far?"

"You're right on the money. But do you know the reason Robertson lied on his report?"

"No. I was hoping you could fill that in."

"Well, it turns out that Robertson and Nick Williams, the only son of Parnell Williams, were lovers back before the war and shacked up together just a block away from the old North Station. Can you believe that?"

"Goodness. How *sordid*." Walter sounded like he was thrilled.

"Sordid isn't all that it is. What I also heard from my source was that Cox, the man who was murdered by Parnell Williams, was lovers with a woman by the name of Marlene Johnson, who was the older man's private secretary. He, meaning Williams, was going to propose to her before he found out she was only in it for his money. It was Cox who killed the daughter, Janet. But when old man Williams found out what Marlene had been up to, he killed her lover out of revenge, both for two-timing him and for killing his kid. What do you think about that?"

Carter was still typing, but he was fuming. He was

positive he knew who'd told Bonnist all those details. There were only four people living (and not in prison) who knew that Dr. Williams had intended to propose to Marlene: Nick, Carter, Mike, and Zelda, the long-time housekeeper who'd worked for Dr. Williams since before Nick's mother had left for Mexico in 1929. Zelda had to be the source.

"I think that's all very interesting, Mr. Bonnist. Now, it's important for me to tell my editor where you got this information so we can verify it."

"Sorry. Ask Lowell Wilson. He'll tell you. I never give up a source."

"Well, I don't know..."

"Look, you work for the *Examiner*! Since when have you used verifiable sources?" Bonnist laughed. "Remember the Spanish-American War and the *Maine*, Mr. Marcello? Mr. Hearst made that one up, didn't he?"

"Well, that was in the *New York Journal-American*—I mean the *Journal*—and it was a very long time ago."

"Times haven't changed *that* much, Mr. Marcello. Lowell Wilson always trusts me. Just ask him."

"I will. If I have any more questions after I do my first draft of the story and run it by my editor, may I phone you again?"

"Of course. Any reporter at the *Examiner* is welcome to call me, day or night. Tell Lowell he still owes me that box of cigars."

"I will. Have a good morning, Mr. Bonnist. And thank you, again."

"Oh, wait just a minute."

"Yes?"

"Are you certain this won't run until Monday?"

"I'm absolutely certain it won't run in Sunday's edition." Carter grinned at that.

"That's good enough for me. And when can I expect

that messenger?"

"Probably late this afternoon. I have a home address for you on California and a business address on Folsom. Which should I use?"

"Use the one on Folsom."

"I will certainly do that. Good day, Mr. Bonnist." Walter put the receiver down on the phone.

Carter hung up Marnie's phone and Sam hung up Nick's. "That was great," said Carter.

Sam put the mic back in Nick's handset. As he did so, he asked, "Do you have any idea who gave him that story?"

Carter nodded and crossed his arms.

"You gonna tell me?"

"Nope. This is a personal matter I have to take care of myself."

"Well," said Sam as he walked over to Marnie's phone and put the mic back inside of her handset, "it would help if we were all playing from the same book."

Carter stood and stretched his arms up towards the ceiling. "I know, but this is one of those things I won't talk about."

Sam shrugged. "You're the boss."

"That's right," said Carter. He looked over at Walter. "Can you arrange for a messenger to send over seventy-five bucks to Bonnist's office?"

"Yes, sir. I was thinking of sending it at 4."

"Good." Carter glanced down at Sam who was frowning. "Walter's bought us some time. What do we do now?"

Sam stood and sighed. "I dunno, bossman. You tell me."

"Sam..."

The older man shook his head and started for the door.

"You can be mad at me all you want," said Carter.

Sam stopped.

"But remember this is about Ferdinand and Gustav and what was done to them in Prague because of this First Secretary person. That's what we need to focus on. We've neutralized Bonnist for the time being. Now we need to deal with Sladek."

Sam, who'd been staring at the front door while Carter had given his little speech, nodded and turned around. He stuffed his hands into his coat pockets and leaned back on his heels. "You're right, Carter. I *am* mad at you for holding out on Walter and me, but Ferdinand and Gustav are what matter here."

"So, what do we do?"

Sam took a deep breath and then gave Carter a lopsided grin. "I think I need to get some air. How's about we meet back up here in time for Walter to dispatch his messenger with Bonnist's dough?"

Carter nodded. "That's fine with me. I have a couple of errands to run."

Sam's eyes darkened in a way Carter had never seen before. It was almost as spooky as when Ferdinand tried to smile. "I'm sure you do," he said. "I'm sure you do."

. . .

Once Sam was gone, Carter looked over at Walter who was staring up at him, owl-like. "One errand I need to run is to go to the bank so we have money for you to give the messenger."

"I never think of you running out of cash."

"Oh! I'm not out. It's just that I'm down to only hundreds at this point."

Walter suddenly snorted with laughter.

"What's so funny?" asked Carter with a grin.

Straightening up and standing up, Walter said, "I

145

guess it's funny to think of needing to go to the bank because you have too much money."

Carter nodded. "I know what you mean. Back before I met Nick, I could've told you my total net worth down to the penny. I knew where every dollar was and how much I had in savings and how much I could spend before payday."

"Wow," said Walter.

"Exactly," replied Carter as he turned off the lights, opened the office door, and led Walter out into the hallway.

. . .

Once they were down on Bush Street, Walter asked, "Which branch are we going to?"

Carter thought for a moment. "Well, there's the one at Geary and Van Ness..."

"Which is a block from McAlister's."

With a laugh, Carter said, "You're right."

"There's the one on Polk, next door to the Royale Theatre."

"You're right," said Carter. He looked at his watch. It was ten past 11. "But there's one at Market, where Geary and Kearny intersect. And I need to get home before Nick wonders what I've been up to."

Walter nodded.

"You wanna walk with me or do you need to be somewhere?"

The shorter man shrugged. "I'll walk with you." He looked around as they started walking downhill towards Powell. "Where's your car?"

"At home," replied Carter as he tipped his hat and stepped aside to let a lady walking uphill to get by. "I dropped it off there and then ran down the hill after we

146

left Ruby's."

"Is that why you were late?"

"Yes," replied Carter as they crossed Powell. "Did you ride with Sam?"

"Yes. He picked me up on the way this morning."

"Do you think he's really mad at me?"

Walter snorted a little. "He was as mad as I've ever seen him when he left."

"He scared me a little."

Walter looked up. "He did?"

With a nod, Carter replied, "He sure did. He's probably the toughest guy we work with."

"Even more than Mr. Robertson?"

"Definitely." Carter added, "Dog shit coming up."

Walter stepped in front of Carter to avoid the mess. "Looks like someone else wasn't so lucky."

"You have a dog or a cat?"

"I have a cat. His name is Mark."

"Mark the cat?" asked Carter with a chuckle.

"He's smart."

"He'd have to be to live with you."

Walter didn't say anything as they walked past the open door of the Owl Market. Carter could smell sausage and onions and oranges, all mixed in, along with some kind of lady's perfume and a strong disinfectant, probably Lysol.

"May I ask you a question, Mr. Jones?" asked Walter after they were across the Stockton Street Tunnel.

"You ever gonna call me Carter?"

"I like to keep professional things on a professional footing."

Carter nodded. "That makes sense." He then stopped to let a woman with a stroller push by. He tipped his hat at her and she smiled, but it was a tired smile, as if she'd done a lot already that morning and had a lot more to do. He then asked, "What's your question?"

"Are you ever jealous of Mr. Robertson?"

Carter laughed. "I thought you liked to keep professional things on a professional footing."

"It is a professional question," retorted Walter. "That is... Well... I mean that I'm talking about the office."

"I see," said Carter.

"More dog poop," announced Walter as he quickly stepped to the side.

That move came so quick that Carter didn't have a chance to stop. He ended up bumping into Walter. To steady himself, he reflexively grabbed Walter's shoulder and squeezed. Once he was steady on his feet again, Carter let go.

Walter looked at his watch. "Wow. I'm late." He quickly turned and jumped out into the street between the nose of an old, gray pre-war Ford coupe and the rear of a brand-new black Cadillac. Waving his arms, he yelled, "Taxi!"

"Walter?" asked Carter.

Keeping his eyes on the traffic heading downhill, Walter said, "I'm sorry, Mr. Jones. I forgot an important appointment." A Veteran's taxi stopped right then. Walter opened the door, saying, "I'll see you at the office at 4." Without waiting for Carter's reply, Walter hopped in the back and slammed the door closed. The cab sped off down Bush and then made a right at the next corner, which was Grant.

Chapter 12: East German spies in San Francisco?

1198 Sacramento Street
San Francisco, Cal.
Friday, November 26, 1954
Half past noon

Carter walked into the kitchen. Everyone, save for Nick, was seated at the table, eating lunch. "What smells so good?"

"Cauliflower soup and fresh bread," announced Mrs. Kopek from her end of the table.

Mrs. Strakova stood, opened the icebox, and pulled out a big slab of something pink that was wrapped in waxed paper. "If you wish, Mr. Carter, I can fry ham."

"Thank you, but soup and bread is fine for me. I had a big breakfast."

She nodded, put the slab back in the icebox, and sat.

Carter walked around to his chair and sat. Mrs. Kopek ladled soup into the bowl sitting in front of his chair. "This is good."

"It smells wonderful."

"What for drink?" asked Gustav.

"Coffee," replied Carter. Looking at Ferdinand, he asked, "Where's Nick?"

"He go office, I think."

"When?"

"Ten minutes ago," replied Mrs. Kopek as she handed the breadbasket to Carter.

Looking over at the bowl sitting in front of Nick's chair, Carter asked, "Did someone call?"

"Yes," replied Mrs. Kopek.

"It was Mr. Mike," added Gustav as he put a mug of coffee down next to Carter's plate.

Carter stood. "Pardon me, y'all. I'll be right back."

. . .

"Yeah?"

"Nick? It's Carter." He was standing at his desk in the office. "They told me I just missed you."

"Yeah," said Nick with a chuckle. "We seem to be doing that a lot today."

"Gustav said Mike called you. Anything wrong?" Carter had decided to get on the phone right away because he was worried that he, Sam, and Walter might have been, somehow, busted.

"Mike's here and was just about to tell me."

"Do you need me to come down?"

Nick said to Mike, "Do we need Carter?"

"No," came the reply. "Tell him this has to do with Hoover."

"Hear that?" asked Nick.

"Yes. Is it bad?"

150

"Is it bad?" relayed Nick.

"Maybe," said Mike. "According to Andy's sources in the Bureau, there are two foreign agents in town. Supposedly, they're looking for Nick. Word straight down the pike from Hoover in D.C. is that the local office is to watch and observe but not to interfere. That has all the G-men here in town in an uproar, as you can imagine."

Nick laughed as Carter whispered, "Damn," into the phone. He didn't know why, but he was positive the two foreign agents were somehow connected to Sladek.

"How foreign?" asked Nick.

Now Mike was laughing. "You won't believe it, but, according to Andy's sources, they're East German."

"You're right. I don't believe you. East German spies in San Francisco? Why?"

"Who knows," replied Mike.

"Are you getting all this, Chief?" asked Nick.

"Yes," replied Carter. He was relieved that they weren't Czechoslovakian, but he wasn't sure that didn't mean they weren't connected to Sladek, though.

"Doesn't that soup smell good?" asked Nick.

"What kinda soup?" asked Mike.

"Cream of cauliflower. And fresh bread."

"I don't know how you two never gain any weight considering you have a French chef cooking for you."

Nick laughed. "Chief?"

"Yes?" Carter was feeling more and more worried by the second. He even looked at the fingernails on his right hand to see if he might want to chew on one. He hadn't bitten his nails since he was a teenager, but it was either that or find one of Nick's cigarettes somewhere. That was how nervous he was feeling.

"Go eat your lunch and tell Mrs. Strakova to save me some. I'm sure I'll be home before too long."

"I will." Carter took in a deep breath. "I love you, Nick."

"I love you, too."

. . .

Carter closed the garden door and then turned to look at Ferdinand and Gustav. He'd stalked back into the kitchen and, somewhat rudely, demanded they follow him outside into the garden so they could talk. "You have got to tell me, Ferdinand. Why don't you want me to tell Nick?"

The man's face turned to stone.

Gustav put his hand on Carter's arm. "Please. We owe Mr. Nick much. This is Czechoslovakian problem, not Mr. Nick problem. He has many problems and—"

Ferdinand grabbed Carter's forearm with his hand and began to turn it slightly. "Mr. Nick no know."

"Ferdinand!" barked Carter. "Stop!"

The other man let go but his stormy face was getting stormier.

Why not just give him a gun? He wants to kill someone. I can see it in his eyes. Better Sladek than me.

Carter shook his head and pushed past those thoughts. "One more time," he said with some heat. "Why don't you want Nick to know?"

Gustav put his hands on his face and started crying.

Putting his arm around his lover, Ferdinand glared at Carter. "He no know. Understand? He no know."

"Why?" asked Carter one last time.

"Many problems," was Ferdinand's only answer as he pulled Gustav into his arms and began to whisper to him soothingly in Czech. The whole time, Ferdinand never once took his eyes off of Carter. The darkness in them was frightening.

. . .

Leaving the two men in the garden, Carter walked through the great room and back towards the office.

Maybe Sam is right. Maybe this has something to do with what the Germans did to them during the war. I was nice and safe and cozy here in San Francisco before, during, and after the war and while all that was happening. Who am I to judge?

Once in the office, Carter closed the door, picked up the phone, and called Sam's number down on Jessie, South of the Slot. He hung up after ten rings. Then he called the number at the apartment that Sam and Ike shared in North Beach. After eleven rings, he hung up again and tried to bite off a corner of his thumbnail, but it was much too thick for him to get anything other than the saltiness of his sweaty hands.

Should I tell Nick? What will that do to Ferdinand? And why did Gustav burst into tears? What is this all about?

Feeling like a caged animal, Carter moved over to the window next to Nick's desk and looked at the green grass of Huntington Park through the sheer curtains.

What about Dr. Williams? Maybe I should go over and talk to him. Lettie might have an idea or two about how to handle this. Maybe she'll know why Ferdinand and Gustav are so damned—

Carter leaned forward. There were two men standing on the sidewalk at the edge of the park. Both were smoking and they were both looking at the house. One appeared to be talking while the other one nodded.

Carter then noticed there was a late-model black Chevrolet parked at the curb right in front of the men. Someone in the car was talking to them. Carter knew that because one of the men kept leaning down slightly to look in the driver's side window. Because of how the car was parked, Carter couldn't see who was behind the wheel, although he knew there was someone there.

Were these the East German agents? Was Sladek the man in the Chevy?

Carter decided to go and find out. He would walk out the door, cross the street as if he were walking across the park to Dr. Williams's apartment, and catch a glance at the man behind the wheel of the Chevrolet. Grabbing a matching hat from the rack by the office door, Carter opened the front door and strode outside onto the porch. He pulled on the hat as he looked out for traffic coming down Sacramento.

From the corner of his eye, Carter saw that the two men had stopped talking and were staring at him.

As soon as a green delivery truck passed by and squealed to a stop at Taylor Street, Carter crossed the street. Remembering something both Nick and Andy had told him, he quickly glanced down at the shoes of the two men and then at the man behind the wheel of the car.

Their shoes gave them away. Carter immediately knew they were Bureau agents. They were probably there doing what Mike had said they'd been instructed to do—watching and observing.

Carter jogged up the steps that led into the park. He stopped about halfway up, snapped his fingers pretending he'd forgotten something, and then jogged back down to the sidewalk. Keeping his eyes on the front door of the house, he abruptly stopped by the trunk of the Chevrolet and turned. "Y'all wouldn't happen to be keeping an eye on us, courtesy of Director Hoover, would you?"

The taller of the pair standing on the sidewalk looked surprised. His partner quietly said, "Move along, Mr. Jones."

Carter took two steps towards the men.

"When a federal agent gives you an order," said the

154

same man in a quiet but determined voice, "I'd advise you to follow it."

Carter glanced at the man behind the wheel and was surprised that his eyes were on the green delivery truck that was still sitting at the corner of Taylor. Carter could see some puffs coming out of the truck's tail pipe, so he knew the engine was on. There was no traffic on Taylor for the driver to wait on, so he had stopped at the curb for some reason. In almost a whisper, Carter asked, "What goes on here?"

"You need to scram," said the shorter man in the same quiet and determined voice.

Carter looked over at Dr. Williams's apartment building across the park and then at the green truck. He wasn't sure what to do.

"You're blowing our cover," said the man.

Carter turned and dashed across the street. Instead of going inside the front door, he decided he would walk past the house and then diagonally across Taylor as if he was going to the grounds of Grace Cathedral. If nothing else, he could walk up the steps to Cathedral House and then survey the scene from there by going inside and coming out just as fast and back over to the house.

That's a terrible idea. Nick would never do something like that.

But, not knowing what else to do, Carter decided to execute his plan. Once his foot was on the curb, he changed his mind, however, and made for the front door of the house. He opened it and, as he did, felt a hand push him from behind as a rough voice said, "Go in, now."

Carter stopped dead, right in the doorway. He slowly turned around and saw two men in strangely tailored brown suits staring up at him. One had a scar across his forehead. Both were about Nick's height and just as thin as him.

"Go," said the one with the scar.

Carter shook his head. "No."

The other one nodded and smiled. It wasn't a creepy smile, although Carter was certain the man thought he was being intimidating. The smile actually lit up his pockmarked face a bit.

"Get off my property."

"No," said the first man, the one with the scar.

Carter just shrugged and, after quickly raising his right hand, made a tight fist and used a move Sugar Joe had taught a long time ago. Aiming for the smiling man's opposite shoulder, as if he was going to slice through his head, Carter brought the blunt side of his hand down at an angle on the man's temple.

The move surprised both men. The one with the scar frowned over at his friend who looked stunned and started wobbling a little.

One... two... three... four...

The smiling man's eyes rolled back into his head as he fell against his friend. If he wasn't dead, which was a distinct possibility, he was going to be out for a while and would wake up feeling like a punch-drunk boxer. Or that was what Sugar Joe had told him would happen.

The man with the scar caught his friend. In an accusing tone, he asked, "What you did?"

Holding up his fist, Carter calmly asked, "You want more of the same?"

Before the man could answer, the two Bureau agents were on the porch. The taller one stepped around and shoved Carter inside the house. Not wanting to be arrested, Carter didn't resist. "Close and lock the door," hissed the man.

Nodding, Carter did just that. Through the window,

he watched as the two Bureau agents carried the stunned man to the green truck. The other man—the one with the scar—stared at Carter through the window for a long moment, before turning and following the agents to the truck. Carter couldn't see the rest of whatever happened, but after a moment, he saw the truck pull away.

He immediately opened the door and ran outside. "Hey!" he yelled.

The two agents were jogging back over to the Chevrolet.

"Hey!" yelled Carter, again, as he ran towards the car.

The men quickly got in and, just as Carter was reaching for one of the doors, the Chevrolet squealed out and sped down Sacramento, blowing through at least three stop signs while Carter watched from the middle of the street.

. . .

Carter was sitting in his leather chair at his desk in the office. He'd closed the door, moved Nick's chair over, and propped it under the knob to keep everyone out.

He was leaning over, holding his handkerchief to his eyes, and silently bawling.

Did I kill that man? What if he has a wife or kids at home? What did I do?

Those words went round and round inside his brain and wouldn't stop. The more he cried, the more the words spun around. The more they spun around, the more he cried.

But the tears were better than the truly devastating thought in the back of his mind. He was crying and worrying about the man he'd just hit to remind himself that he wasn't his father.

He didn't want to see in his mind what he'd seen his father do with his eyes. He didn't want to hear the jeers of the crowd and their taunts. He didn't want to smell the urine and the shit coming from the trousers of the colored man who was swinging from the tree.

The man whose name Carter had never heard. The man their father had brought Carter and Bobby to see as if they were going to see the circus.

The harder he cried and the more he worried about the bereaved wife and the fatherless children, the less he had to notice how much he was like his father.

Why did I have to hit him like that? He didn't have a gun. He didn't have the strength to do anything to me other than bat at me like a kid trying to push away an elephant.

That silly thought broke the spell. Carter took a deep breath, wiped his eyes and his face, and then blew his nose.

I need to talk to Sam.

. . .

On the fifth ring, Carter heard Sam say, "Hello?"

"It's Carter."

Sam sighed. "I'm really sorry. I can get like that sometimes."

"No, Sam, I'm sorry."

With a chuckle, Sam said, "Now that we're buddies again, I'd suck your dick to make it up to you, but I don't think Nick would like that." Before Carter could say anything to that preposterous idea, Sam plowed on. "Did you take care of it, whatever it was?"

Carter snorted into the phone. "No. I didn't get a chance. We have a *huge* problem."

"What?"

158

"I think I may have just killed an East German foreign agent."

"What!" exploded Sam.

Carter recounted the events of the last hour or so.

"You *have* to show me that move."

"No!" barked Carter. "I probably killed the man. I hit him right on the temple."

"Is that bothering you?" asked Sam in a quiet voice. He sounded just like Gustav right then. His American accent had disappeared.

"It sure the hell is."

"Carter, my friend, listen to me. You are protecting your house and your family. This man was there to take away Ferdinand, who is part of your family." Sam cleared his throat as if he could suddenly hear himself speaking. Sounding more like an American, he continued, "Why do you think they showed up with a truck? Do you think they were to deliver flowers? They wanted to grab Ferdinand and take him back to Prague. You did good, Carter."

Carter looked down at his desk. He wasn't sure he believed what Sam was saying.

Sam continued, "We need to—"

"No! I'm not telling Nick. You're right, Sam. He's family. I don't understand why Ferdinand and Gustav want to keep this quiet and under wraps, but I saw what you were talking about."

"They're wounded. They were too young for the war, but they might as well be walking around with shrapnel inside. It scares me sometimes. I wonder what Ferdinand might be capable of."

I could say the same thing about you... And I have.

Carter heard someone turning the office door and trying to push it open.

"Mr. Carter?" It was Gustav.

In a whisper, Carter said, "Gotta go, Sam. See you at the office at 4."

"What about Mike and Nick?"

Carter thought for a moment.

Gustav pushed against the door. "Mr. Carter?"

"Hold on!"

Sam laughed. "Do you have Nick's chair pushed under the doorknob?"

"Yes," replied Carter. "If I'm not downstairs in front of the building, come on up. I'll go over early. If I can't get rid of them, I'll meet you on the sidewalk."

"Fine. And Carter?"

"Yes?"

"Don't give yourself a hard time. You did what you had to do."

"Thanks." Carter sighed as he hung up the phone.

. . .

Having moved Nick's chair out of the way, Carter opened the door. Before a worried Gustav could say anything, Nick breezed his way around the corner with a big smile. "Hiya, Chief!"

Trying to smile back, Carter replied, "Hi, Nick."

Gustav slipped away right then.

Nick stepped forward. "Mrs. Strakova is heating up some soup for me." Rubbing his hands together, "After I eat, do you wanna take a drive up out to the beach?"

With a quick glance at his watch (it was 1:25), Carter said, "I have a better idea."

"What's that?"

"Let's you and me go to Playland."

"Playland?" Nick was frowning.

Carter rubbed his hands together. "Sure. I never had lunch either and, ever since Henry mentioned them yesterday, I've had a hankering for hot dogs and a Coke and maybe a ride on the tilt-a-whirl." He wanted to get out of the house in case the one East German agent came back with reinforcements. Also, Carter needed to get out and away from everything for a little while before he lost his mind.

"You're kidding, right?"

"No. I was thinking how we've never been there, and I know you and Janet liked that place when you were kids."

"Because we were kids. Do adults go there by themselves?"

Carter shrugged. "I don't know. But what I do know is I want a hot dog." He glanced at his watch again. *Time for another lie.* "And I have an appointment with Chief Morris in San Mateo at the Humboldt Street station at 5 to give an hour's talk on arson investigation."

"At 5 on a Friday?"

Carter nodded. "The chief just called and asked if I could come down. I know it's short notice, but he's got the 6 pm crew coming in an hour early."

Nick shrugged. "I'm always up for a hot dog. Instead of Playland, how about we go to a stand I've been to before?" He frowned up at Carter. "Have you been crying, Chief?"

Carter felt like he'd been caught. He blushed and nodded and said the first thing that occurred to him. "I was thinking about Bobby and how much I miss him."

Nick stared into his eyes for a moment. Then, he smiled a little and said, "The guy I know has a cart right by Aquatic Park. We can grab a cab, so we don't have to worry about parking. It outta be kinda busy up there. Would you like that?"

Suddenly feeling better about the whole mess, Carter reached his arms around his husband and pulled him in close. "Nicholas Williams, you seriously wanna be a tourist?"

"Yeah," replied Nick in a muffled voice because his face was buried in Carter's chest, something that always made Carter inexplicably happy.

. . .

They were all standing in the kitchen. Everyone except Nick, of course. Carter had told him he would break the bad news to Mrs. Strakova that they didn't want her soup for lunch. That was just a ruse to let everyone else know what was going on. Based on Gustav's expression earlier, Carter knew they'd heard the fracas at the front door.

Looking around at everyone, Carter said, "Nick is on the phone and I just have a couple of minutes before he'll come looking for me."

"What happen at door?" asked Gustav.

"There were two men from East Germany who were probably here for you two."

"*Germans*," hissed Ida venomously.

Gustav seriously blanched and glanced at Ferdinand who simply looked like he was ready to commit murder right then and there.

"I don't think they'll be back." Carter bit his lip. "I may have accidentally killed one of them, though."

Mrs. Strakova (who knew a thing or two about murdering Germans from when she lived in Paris during the war) clapped her hands together and smiled while the others all just stared up at Carter, their eyes wide in admiration. Even Ferdinand looked less murderous. Mrs. Kopek, however, was dabbing her eyes with a handkerchief.

"We're going out for a while," said Carter. He looked

at Gustav. "You two stay out of sight. Do not answer the door."

The man nodded.

"Mrs. Kopek?"

"Yes, Mr. Carter?"

"If anyone knocks on the door, don't open it. Tell them through the glass that everyone is gone."

She nodded.

"We'll be back around 3:45 or so. Then I'm meeting Sam and Walter at the office to take care of something that will, hopefully, get us closer to ending all of this."

"I will go New York," announced Ferdinand for no good reason.

Gustav sighed heavily while Mrs. Kopek chastised Ferdinand in Czech.

"No," said Carter. "No one is going anywhere. Let Sam and Walter and me take care of this."

Ferdinand hissed. "Mr. Nick no know."

Throwing his hands up in the air in frustration, Carter said, "OK! I'm lying to my husband and to Mike. Because if I don't tell Nick, I'm not telling Mike. All of this will get me in a lot of trouble." He looked around the assembled group. "Can anyone here explain why?"

Ferdinand looked at the floor.

"He has many problems," muttered Gustav.

Carter looked at Mrs. Kopek. "Can you explain this?"

She shook her head. "I do not understand."

Ida stomped her foot and crossed her arms. "Mr. Nick save us."

Nora, Gustav, and Ferdinand all nodded.

"So, you want me to save Nick from... what?" He tried to wrap his head around the whole thing (one more time) while secretly hoping Nick would burst into the kitchen.

"Yes," said Gustav.

Mrs. Strakova put her hand on Carter's arm. "You do not understand how it was in the war."

Carter nodded. "I know I don't." He looked at Mrs. Kopek. "Do you?"

She shook her head and dabbed her eyes again. "We were lucky to be here in San Francisco."

Nick pushed open the kitchen the door right then. "Chief?"

Everyone scattered like mice. Most of them went down to their rooms under the kitchen.

Nick grinned. "Everything OK?"

Putting on a smile, Carter nodded. "We're wrapping up that *thing*."

Ferdinand, who was standing by the door that led down to the garage, suddenly stopped and turned. He silently marched over to Nick and hugged him tightly.

Patting the man on the back, Nick asked, "What's this?"

"I love you, Mr. Nick."

Glancing at Carter over Ferdinand's shoulder with a grin, Nick said, "I love you too. We both do."

"Yes, Mr. Carter is..." Ferdinand choked. He then let go of Nick and ran over to the door. He opened it and dashed down the stairs.

"What was that about?"

Carter shrugged.

Chapter 13: Hot dogs by the bay.

At Hyde and Beach
San Francisco, Cal.
Friday, November 26, 1954
About half past 2 in the afternoon

As Carter wolfed down his second foot-long, he looked at Nick. They were sitting on a bench on the north side of Beach and watching the sailboats out on the bay.

"It's good, right?" asked Nick as he handed Carter another paper napkin.

"Sure is, Boss. I can't imagine Playland would have any better."

Nick sighed, crossed his legs, and looked out at the bay.

"How do you know about this guy?" Carter was referring to the man who'd sold them two regular coneys (for Nick), two foot-longs (for Carter), and two bottles of Coke.

"I was working a case around here in '52."

"Anything interesting?"

"Not really. Usual story. This guy thought his wife was cheating. He wanted a divorce, and she wouldn't do him the favor and drive up to Reno." Nick looked over at Carter. "I'm sure I told you about this one."

"Maybe," replied Carter before continuing to inhale his food.

"Well, I found out she was cheating on him. To be honest, I never understood why. Her husband—my client—looked like a mix between you and Sam. He was about my height but solid and muscled."

"Physical culture?"

Nick laughed and pulled on his ankle. "No. He used to work in the oil patch down around Bakersfield and, since they got married and moved up here, had bought a warehouse and wasn't afraid to help his guys out."

"Sounds like a good man."

"He was. He paid me five hundred up front and didn't cry when I gave him the evidence."

Carter crumpled his paper wrapper and handed it to Nick to put in the paper bag they were using for garbage. "What was the other guy like?"

Nick hooked his thumb over his shoulder. "He worked for Ghirardelli as an accountant. He was just a pasty-faced paper pusher. She would meet him over here for lunch when the weather was nice. I even caught them on camera doing some light macking. I never understood the appeal."

"Maybe he had hidden talents," whispered Carter.

Nick chuckled. "Could be. He was a little taller than me and pretty lanky."

"What does your vast study of sailors tell you about that?"

Nick burst out laughing. "My experience in the Navy would seem to indicate that it might have gone all the way to his knee." Nick glanced over at Carter. "You know, for your build, you're an exception."

Carter crossed his arms as his face started burning with embarrassment. He liked his equipment and knew how to use it but didn't like talking about it. "Good to know."

Nick chuckled a little and then uncrossed his legs.

Once he was recovered, Carter asked, "Did they ever get divorced?"

"Yeah. And the funny thing is she went up to Reno after all."

"How do you know that?"

"Because I saw a blurb about her wedding to the accountant in the *Chronicle* two months later."

"How do you know she went to Reno?"

"California divorces take six months, not six weeks."

Carter nodded. "Gotcha."

"If I'd known the weather was gonna be this nice, I would've called Captain O'Reilly so we could take the ship out on the bay."

Carter looked over and smiled. "I'm glad we came here. Feels like a normal day."

Nodding, Nick smiled back. "It does. We don't have as many of those as we used to, do we?"

Tell him. Just tell him. Stop lying. Stop pretending everything is normal.

To clear his head, Carter looked out at the water and then over at the Golden Gate Bridge. He remembered those days, back before the war, when he and Henry would spend a lazy Sunday afternoon walking across the bridge and back. It was a cheap thrill.

I killed a man today.

Carter abruptly stood.

"Chief?" asked Nick. "You OK?"

Afraid to look at his husband, Carter said, "Just tired of sitting."

"Let me put this in that trash barrel over there and

167

then we can walk down to the beach in the cove."

I can't keep doing this. It's gonna eat me alive from the inside. I'm a murderer.

Carter put his hand over his face.

When Hoover finds out, they'll come and arrest me.

He removed his hand and, terrified, stared at the white stone prison on Alcatraz Island.

That's where I'll be. I'll be looking over here and remembering the best hot dogs I've ever had. And Nick and how much I love him and how I'll never see him again.

"Carter?" Nick was right at his elbow and speaking softly. "Still thinking about Bobby?"

It's lying time again.

"Yes."

Nick took a deep breath. "Does this have anything to do with what you and Louise talked about yesterday?"

Confused, Carter looked down at Nick. "What?"

"I saw you. She seemed to be laying down the law about something and you were obviously upset." Nick hesitated and then continued, "You get moody like this whenever you spend time with her."

Isn't Nick the best husband, ever? He even gives me the lines I need so I can lie to him.

Carter tentatively nodded. "Maybe."

Turning to look at the bay, Nick said, "She needs to get married to someone who really loves her."

Those words hit Carter hard. Tears ran down his cheeks as he quickly pulled out his handkerchief so no one would see a grown man cry on a beautiful San Francisco day.

Chapter 14: Sam tells it like it is.

Offices of Consolidated Security, Inc.
777 Bush Street
San Francisco, Cal.
Friday, November 26, 1954
Just before 4 in the afternoon

Carter was sitting at Nick's desk, feeling the devastation that hadn't stopped since he'd started crying at the Aquatic Park when the door opened and Sam, followed by Walter, walked into the office.

Sam took one look at Carter and started frowning. "What's wrong?"

Carter started working his jaw and shaking his head. "I can't fucking do this."

Walking over, Sam stood next to him, took off Carter's hat, and placed it on the desk. Pulling Carter's head to his muscled belly, Sam said, "You didn't kill the poor slob. I called around and found out what happened. His buddy dropped him off at Saint Francis

Hospital and then a G-man showed up and arrested him for espionage. He'll live but he won't be happy about it."

Carter looked up.

With a silly smile, Sam put his finger on Carter's nose. "Red, you're not a murderer."

Carter chuckled and buried his face in Sam's coat and shirt. The man smelled like sweat and something spicy.

After a moment, Sam patted his back. "You keep doin' that, Carter Jones, and I'm gonna have to strip off all your clothes so I can have my way with you."

Walter snorted from the other side of the room as Carter pulled away. Walter then asked, "Do you have the cash, Mr. Jones?"

Sam walked over and sat down in the chair across from Nick's desk while Carter pulled out his wallet. "Here's three twenties, a ten, and two fives. I figured there was a fee."

Walter nodded as he walked over and cautiously took the cash from Carter's outstretched hand. He looked like was taking something from a lion or an alligator or some other big and dangerous beast.

That's how he sees Mike and me. We're just big beasts and he might get trampled.

Carter realized he was right. That was exactly how Walter saw the two of them. That was why he was always so cautious around them. Carter didn't blame him. If he was that short and slight, he might feel the same way.

Looking at the money in his hand, Walter said, "I guess maybe I should start keeping a parallel set of books for things like this."

"Like what?" asked Sam, as he put his feet up on Nick's desk.

With a shrug, Walter said, "This thing we're doing."

He looked at Carter. "You know this is likely going to happen again, right, Mr. Jones?"

"No, Walter," replied Carter, suddenly irritated. "I don't know that at all."

Sam grinned over his shoes. "You know he's right. That's why it's bugging the shit outta you right now."

Carter cleared his throat. "I don't know what you're talking about."

"I'm going down to my office to call the messenger service," said Walter before letting himself out into the hallway.

"Red, I don't think you're cut out for this kinda stuff," said Sam, stilling looking at Carter over his shoes.

Don't kill the employees. Don't kill the employees.

Carter took a deep breath. "Why not?" he asked before quickly adding, "What kinda stuff do you mean?"

"You need to stick to arson investigating. Let the rest of us do the big stuff."

Furious, Carter was on his feet in a flash. "Fuck you!"

Pulling a cigar out of his coat pocket, Sam lazily asked, "Have a lighter or a match?"

Carter crossed his arms and shook his head.

With a sigh, Sam pulled his feet of Nick's desk and stood. He walked over to Marnie's desk and began to rifle through her drawers. "Found one," he said as held up a box of matches. He bit off one end of the cigar and spit that into the garbage pail. He then lit a match and held it for a long moment as he puffed on the cigar to get it to light. He then blew out the match and walked over to Nick's desk where he dropped it in an ashtray. He looked at Carter for a long moment before saying, "The trouble with you is that you're too honest."

"What does that mean?"

Sam examined the lit end of his cigar for a moment. "If Nick was my man and Ferdinand worked for me, you can bet Hans would be dead and not handcuffed to a hospital bed right now."

"Hans? Who's Hans?"

"Hans, Fritz, Adolph... whatever his name is. That agent you clocked. I would have gone in for the kill." He tried to puff on his cigar, but nothing happened. He looked at the end of it again. With a frown, he said, "The damn things never stay lit." He turned and walked back to Marnie's desk for another match.

"Are you telling me that you'd kill someone that easily?"

"Easy?" asked Sam as he lit a second match. After he'd gotten the cigar to light, he said, "Easy ain't the point. The man was after one of yours. Like the English say, you're the Lord of the Manor. It's yours to protect."

"That house belongs to Nick."

"Bull... shit..." said Sam as he dropped his match in the ashtray on Nick's desk. "You're the reason he lives there."

"What do you mean?"

"I know the story, Carter. You're the one who made up with the old man. You're the one who got them back together last Christmas. You're the reason you now live in that house." He puffed hard on the cigar, but, again, nothing happened. "When you buy cheap, you get cheap," he noted before putting the cigar on the edge of Nick's desk.

"That's the second time you've said that about me being the reason we live on Sacramento Street."

Sam walked around the desk and got right up close to Carter. Looking up, he said, "Doncha see? The old man would've never left if there wasn't anyone to give the place to. Even after he married Leticia, he didn't need a place that big."

"Nick and I don't need a place that big," said Carter, realizing that wasn't that point but wanting to get that on the record, so to speak.

Sam laughed. He reached up and pinched Carter's cheek. "Sure you do. Do you think the richest men in the City can live in Eureka Valley? The old man was just bowing to the inevitable. You and Nick belong there. It's your castle. And you gotta defend it, Red."

"Stop calling me that."

Sam turned on his heels, walked around the desk, and sat down. "Better than calling you what you really are, which is nothing but a juvenile. You're just a baby when it comes to the rough-and-tumble of dealing with what's really going on around Nick." He laughed. "Mike tells all of us all the time that our main job is to protect Nick. Why do you think Walter and me are involved in this? It's *our* job. And it's *your* job, too, Red. It will be until the day one of you kicks the bucket."

Carter knew Sam was right even if he didn't like the way he was saying what he was saying.

"Your problem is you're a golden boy." Sam grinned. "You have no idea how many kids I've known just like you. Moscow was filled with golden boys, all fresh in from the countryside and ready to make the revolution a going proposition. Of course, most of 'em are dead now because if there was one thing Stalin couldn't stand it was idealism." He grabbed his cigar from the edge of the desk and looked at it again. "He killed them all. Had 'em murdered. Artists, intellectuals, Army officers, you name it. If they didn't bow down to him, he had them killed." Sam pointed the unlit cigar at Carter. "You're just like one of those golden boys running around Moscow in the 20s. Your idealism is gonna get you killed. You better wise up, Carter Jones. Nick can afford to walk around with his head in the clouds like he does, making sure no one in San Francisco goes hungry if he can help it or whatever his charity of the moment happens to be, but you gotta do your job and you job is to keep Nick alive. That's all our jobs."

"You make this sound like a religion."

Sam jumped up with a big grin on his face. "Of course! It's the New Church of Nick Williams. He's the homosexual who'll save the world. And he'll save you, too, Carter, but you gotta keep him alive."

"How?"

"Be willing to kill for him."

Carter shook his head. "I don't believe any of this."

With a shrug, Sam walked over towards the office door. He put his hand on the doorknob, but then stopped.

"You're crazy," said Carter, realizing he was probably more right than not.

Sam turned and looked at Carter from across the room. "I am *not* crazy." He sounded like Gustav. "But I am older than you and have been to some dark places I hope you never see." He cleared his throat and resumed talking in his American accent. "And to be honest, I don't care if you believe me or agree with me or whether you wanna kick me down the stairs to the street and tell me to fuck off and never come back." He smiled in a way that was hard to look at. "I'm a convert now. It's Saint Nick for me all the way, Red. Until the day I die, I'll be looking out for him. Believe me." He turned, opened the door, and left.

Carter did believe him. That was the scary part.

. . .

Walter walked back into the office less than a minute later. "Where is Mr. Halversen going?"

"I don't know and I don't care," replied Carter who was still standing next to Nick's chair. "Did you call the messenger service?"

"Yes. They'll be here in about fifteen minutes to pick up this." He held out a brown envelope.

"Thank you, Walter." Carter took a deep breath and sat down in Nick's chair. "I hope you know how much I appreciate all your help with this."

Walter walked over to the desk. "It's my pleasure, Mr. Jones. I hope you know I would do anything for you and Mr. Williams."

Carter didn't like the sound of that on the heels of what Sam had just said, but he knew Walter didn't mean those words in the same way, so he smiled. "Thank you, Walter."

"Now that we know Mr. Bonnist won't go to the *Examiner*, at least until there's no story on Monday, what do we do next?"

Good question. Too bad I'm too scared to ask Sam the same thing.

"How about we re-group in the morning?" suggested Carter. "We still have a couple of days to sort this out."

Walter nodded. "Sometimes a good night's sleep can help."

Carter grinned. "I hope so. In the meantime, I'm thinking I might take Nick out to Ernie's tonight for steaks and then get us both good and drunk. How about you?"

Walter looked at Nick's desk. "I have a date, but I'm, uh, not sure I should keep it."

"Oh? Who with?"

"It's no one you know, Mr. Jones." Walter was still looking at Nick's desk. "I met him, um, a couple of

175

weeks ago at a house party on Russian Hill. He phoned me Tuesday night and invited me to dinner."

"Where's he taking you?"

Walter blushed. "I don't really know."

"I hope you have a good time."

"I don't know if, uh, I should, you know, keep the date or not."

Carter leaned forward a little. "Can I help?"

Shaking his head emphatically, Walter said, "I don't think so." He then looked over at Carter. "Uh, what time is Mr. Williams expecting you back?"

Looking at his watch (it was a 4:50), Carter said, "Not until 7 or so. Why? Do you wanna grab a beer somewhere?"

Walter's eyes widened in alarm. "Oh, no, Mr. Jones, but thank you for the offer."

Carter smiled. "Sure."

"I was just wondering because, you know, if you were really going to San Mateo, you might wanna call the fire department to see if there are any fires, you know, before you go home."

Carter sat back, slightly appalled at Walter's deviousness but also admiring how smart the man was and how he was thinking through all the angles. "Good idea." Carter leaned forward to pick up the phone so he could call Information.

"Oh, no, Mr. Jones. Let me call."

With a grin, Carter put the phone down. "Fine. Thanks, Walter."

. . .

Walter was sitting at Robert's desk and was on the phone, pencil and pad at the ready. "Hello, Operator. I'd like the main number for the San Mateo Fire Department, please." He nodded and started writing.

176

"Diamond 3-3611. Is that correct?" Pause. "Thank you." He reached and pressed the switch hook on the phone.

He then dialed the seven numbers and waited. "Yes, this is Walter Marcello with the *San Francisco Examiner* and I'm calling to check on the current status of activity of the fire department before we finish our final edition for the day." He waited and listened. Then he made a note on the pad and said, "Thank you. To confirm: the truck company from the Humboldt station is on call now at a fire on Railroad Avenue. Do you know the name of the business?" He made another note. "West Coast Container at number 25. Any idea whether arson is involved?" He nodded. "Yes, of course. I understand. Thank you for your help. Goodbye."

Walter hung up the phone and smiled over at Carter who was sitting in Marnie's chair. "I think you need to go home, Mr. Jones. Your arson lecture has been interrupted by a suspected arson fire." He laughed to himself as he tore the three top pages off the notepad he'd been using and ran his finger over the blank page that remained on top. He then tore off two more sheets, folded them all up, and stuffed them in his coat pocket.

"Thanks, Walter. What are you doing with those pieces of paper?"

"Removing any trace of my writing."

Carter nodded, duly impressed. Once again.

Chapter 15: An abrupt conclusion.

1198 Sacramento Street
San Francisco, Cal.
Saturday, November 27, 1954
Just past dawn

Carter opened his eyes and then closed them again. The light leaking in around the curtains was too painful. Running his tongue over the inside of his mouth, he wondered why he'd forgotten to take any aspirin before collapsing into bed earlier that morning.

He'd taken Nick to Ernie's and the two had started off dinner with a bottle of French champagne. Nick had switched to Martinis while Carter had started guzzling bourbon. After dinner, they'd walked down Montgomery and into the Black Cat. They didn't know the performer that night, but they'd been mobbed by people they hadn't seen in years. Carter spent a lot of the evening try to keep guys from sitting on his lap, something that Nick thought was absurdly funny.

By midnight, they'd had enough of the crowd and

stumbled out to find a cab. Carter had given the guy their home address, but Nick had insisted he wanted to go to the Silver Rail on Market, which was a real dive bar. There they ran into some guys who claimed to know them both but neither could remember. Nick, of course, had bought three rounds for the whole bar. That was much to the delight of the bartenders to whom he gave several hundred dollars in tips—basically emptying his wallet. Carter paid for the final cab ride home with one of his hundreds. That fact earned him help with Nick who had passed out before they got up to Nob Hill.

The cabbie got so excited when he realized he would get to see "the inside of a real-live Nob Hill mansion," that his oohing and aahing woke up Gustav who took one look and disappeared. He then reappeared with Ferdinand who unceremoniously kicked the cabbie out of the house and got him on his way to his next fare.

Ferdinand had then carried Nick upstairs, something Carter would have normally done if he'd been able to stand up straight, which he couldn't. Ferdinand and Gustav got Nick undressed while Carter got sick in the bathroom. Once he was all done with that, Ferdinand helped him get undressed and put him to bed with a kiss on the forehead.

Or, at least, that was what Carter remembered as he stumbled out of bed and into the bathroom to relieve himself and get a couple of glasses of water before crawling back into bed.

. . .

The next time Carter opened his eyes, he felt a little better. He also smelled breakfast, particularly bacon. Sitting up just a little, he looked around. Nick was still asleep on his left. Ferdinand was helping Gustav set up plates of food in front of the Chesterfield.

"Morning," said Carter, surprised he could speak.

"Good morning," replied Gustav with a smile.

"Yes. Good morning," added Ferdinand who was smiling as much as he ever did without looking creepy.

"You two look cheery."

"Good news," said Ferdinand as he stood at the end of the bed.

"Very good news," added Gustav.

"What?" asked Carter.

Gustav brought over some clothes for Carter to put on (he and Nick always slept in the buff) and said, "I will tell you in other room. Ferdinand will wake Mr. Nick."

. . .

Carter was sitting on Nick's old bed in his childhood bedroom staring at the front page of the *Examiner* that Gustav had just handed him.

"Where'd you get this?" asked Carter. That newspaper was not normally allowed in the house.

"I get at store."

"Why?"

"Mrs. Kopek tell me."

"What am I looking for?" asked Carter as he yawned.

Gustav walked over and pointed to a headline just under the fold. "This."

CITY PEDS MEET END

Two men in separate sections of the city yesterday both met their deaths while crossing busy streets.

David Bonnist, 39, was killed at approximately 7 p.m. last night by an unknown hit-and-run driver who was making a right turn onto 9th Ave as Bonnist crossed Irving St in the Sunset District. Witnesses say a battered black Chevrolet possibly a '36 or '37 ran the red light as Bonnist was crossing presumably to catch the "N" streetcar. Police identified Bonnist thanks to his private investigation license in his pocket. He had offices on Folsom St in the Mission District and lived with his wife and their three children on California St. His father-in-law is Peter O. Webb, founder and president of California Amalgamated Insurance.

Alexander Sladek was killed when he fell into the path of an oncoming truck late last evening just before 10 p.m. on California St near Grant. Sladek was identified as being employed by the Czechoslovakian Consulate in New York City. He was reported to be in the City as part of a group of Red consular officials touring the west coast. Police did not charge the truck driver, Robert Martinez of San Francisco, as he was observed by witnesses to be following all traffic laws when the unfortunate incident occurred.

Carter looked up at Gustav. He felt sick to his stomach. He knew Sam was somehow involved in both accidents. They were too convenient to be coincidental. And it matched what Sam had said about "Saint Nick."

"May I have?" asked Gustav as he held out his hand.

Nodding silently, Carter handed over the section he was holding.

Gustav turned a few pages and then folded the paper over and handed it back. He pointed to a small article at the bottom. "Read here."

CZECH RED OFF TO RUSS

NEW YORK, Nov. 27.—(AP) — Czechoslovakia First Sec'y Antonin Novotny canceled plans today for U.N. tour in N.Y. scheduled to begin Monday. Novotny will be attending a private consult with Soviet officials in Moscow prior to attending a security summit there in early December. Members of the 7 Eastern European Communist nations will convene over concerns about possible W. German rearmament, now being discussed by Adenauer government in Bonn.

Feeling hollow, Carter looked up. "This says he canceled his trip yesterday."

Nodding, Gustav said, "Yes. This is good, no?"

No, this is terrible.

"We throw big party on Monday for Mr. Nick for birthday."

Nick was turning 32 and was not a fan of birthday parties. But Carter was too wrapped up in his horror about what Sam had done to do more than say, "Oh, sure."

"Mrs. Strakova make lasagna and big cake." Gustav smiled. "No garlic for you."

Carter nodded absently. "No garlic for me."

. . .

"Chief?"

Carter looked over at Nick. They were sitting on

184

opposite ends of the Chesterfield in front of the fire while plowing through a mound of bacon and eggs. "Yes, Boss?"

"That was a lot of fun last night."

Carter smiled a little. "It was."

Looking down at his plate, Nick quietly said, "None of this has anything to do with Bobby, does it?"

I knew it! I must have told when I was drunk last night. Damn it!

"What do you mean?"

Nick frowned a little. "When Jeffery and I were together, every now and then he would take me out for a big blow-out like you did last night." He put his plate down on the coffee table and then turned to face Carter. "What's really wrong?"

Carter stared into Nick's milk chocolate eyes and tried to figure out what to say. Even though it had been several hours since the last time Ferdinand had tried to threaten him into silence, Carter doubted that what was in the newspaper meant they would now be OK with him spilling the beans. Then he had an idea...

Carter leaned forward and put down his plate, as well. He wiped off his fingers with his napkin and scooted over to Nick's end of the Chesterfield. Putting his arm around his husband's shoulder, he began to tell a part of the truth of what had been going on. "I can't tell you how I know this, but I found out something about Mike and your father that's been weighing heavy on my mind."

Nick buried his face into his neck. "What?"

"If I tell you, you can't tell anyone. Promise?"

"Sure."

"Mike lied on the incident report he filed."

"When Father killed that Marty?"

"Yes. Mike said that Marty committed suicide and

185

then his captain convinced the D.A. to give Marlene a reduced sentence down in Chino in exchange for her keeping quiet."

Nick sighed. "I figured he'd done something like that."

"You did?"

"Yeah. It all went away so easily. Did you notice that it disappeared from the papers? There was just a little item in the *Chronicle* when Marlene was sentenced. That was it."

"When did that happen?"

"While we were in Washington, D.C. Marnie cut it out and saved it for me. That's how I know."

"Oh," replied Carter, feeling tremendously relieved.

"Is that what's been bothering you these last couple of days?"

"Yes."

You're lying, son.

Nick pulled back and looked up with a concerned frown. "Why was it bothering you so much?"

"I was afraid you might get mad at Mike, I guess." Carter quickly added, "And I don't want your father to know."

"Me, neither."

Carter reached over and gently bit Nick on the ear. There was something about doing so that made Carter both happy and horny.

"Are you serious?" asked Nick.

"About what?"

"You just bit my ear."

Carter chuckled. "How's your headache?"

"Not bad enough to push you outta bed, that's for sure."

Carter quickly stood, reached down, and picked up Nick. He carried his husband over to the bed and threw him down like he was a sack of potatoes. It had its usual effect on Nick down south of the border and that made Carter very happy, indeed.

Epilogue: Wrapping up loose ends.

1198 Sacramento Street
San Francisco, Cal.
Saturday, November 27, 1954
Later that morning

Carter was jogging down the stairs when he heard Nick call out, "Chief?" He turned around and headed back upstairs.

Nick was standing in the hallway without a stitch of clothes but wearing a big grin on his face. "Don't forget. We're gonna meet Captain O'Reilly at the marina at noon to go out on the bay."

Carter smiled. "I know."

"This secret mission you're on better not having anything to do with my birthday."

"That's for me to know and you to find out."

Nick tried to look tough. "Chief..."

Carter shrugged, turned around, and said, "See you at noon, sailor!"

. . .

Carter got out of the Veteran's Cab across the street from the front of 2111 Hyde at the corner of Filbert. He looked at his watch. It was almost 9.

He waited for a car to go by and then dashed across Hyde and up the steps to the lobby of the six-story apartment building. A man in a blue uniform standing behind a counter asked, "May I help you?"

"I'm here to see Zelda Markinson, please."

"Is she expecting you?"

Carter shook his head. "No. You can tell her it's Carter Jones. I think she'll see me."

The man's eyebrows went up as he recognized the name. With a slight shrug, he picked up a telephone under the counter and pressed a button.

. . .

When Carter got off the elevator on the fifth floor, Zelda was standing just outside her apartment door at the far end of the hall. She didn't smile and she didn't say anything. She just waited for him to get to where she was and then led him inside. Carter closed the door and followed her past the kitchen and into the living room.

"Please, make yourself at home," said Zelda. "Would you like a cup of coffee? Or some tea? I have a pot steeping."

"No, thank you."

She pointed at the window and said, "Have a look," before turning and going into the kitchen.

Carter walked over to the big window. She had a southern view. Since the building was on the southern edge of Russian Hill, he could see the Huntington Hotel and part of Grace Cathedral. He could also see the roof of 1198 Sacramento and the big window at the far end of the attic. It was mildly disturbing that she had an unobstructed view of the place where she'd once worked for over 25 years.

After a moment, she returned with a pretty teacup on a delicate saucer. "Why are you here?" She looked calm as a cucumber, but Carter was sure she was terrified. It was something about the way her eyes darted all over his face.

"You told a private investigator about what really happened the day Marty Cox was shot in the library. Didn't you?"

She blinked twice and then put her teacup and saucer on a bookshelf piled with knickknacks. "Yes." Her eyes relaxed and she stared right into his.

"Why? Did he pay you?"

She smiled just a little. "Why should I tell you?"

Carter realized she had a point. He wasn't even sure what he was doing there.

As if reading his mind, she asked, "What did you think I would do if you asked me?" Her smile widened. "Start crying? Beg your forgiveness?" She took a deep breath and shook her head. "No, Mr. Jones, I owe you nothing."

"Then why did you let me come up?"

"I wanted to know what you wanted." She stood up completely straight in a way that reminded Carter of her well-deserved nickname "Zelda the Indomitable." She pointed towards the hall. "Now that I know, I'll ask you to kindly leave before I phone the police."

Carter looked at her for a long moment and then walked down the hall, through the door, and to the elevator.

. . .

191

He was back in front of Zelda's building, looking for a cab when he heard a man behind him say, "Gotta light, buddy?"

Carter turned and saw that one of the Bureau agents from the day before was standing there, looking up at him with an unlit cigarette in the corner of his mouth and smiling. "No," replied Carter, as he looked up Hyde to see if a cab was coming. He didn't see one.

"That's too bad," said the agent. "But it's lucky I ran into you."

"Lucky?"

"You see today's papers?" The man folded his arms. "Seems like you've been lucky in all sorts of ways."

"Really?" Carter was still scanning the street. Nothing yet. He was prepared to start running down Filbert or Hyde to get away from the man if he had to. But he figured that, being a federal agent, the man was probably carrying a gun.

If he wants me dead, there's probably not anything I can do.

"Yeah. You and Mr. Williams got *real* lucky. Kinda coincidental, doncha think?" The man took the cigarette out of the corner of his mouth and dropped it in his coat pocket. "I mean, how often is it that all the people who are harassing you drop off the face of the Earth just like that?" He snapped his fingers. "Let's see. We got two foreign agents and—"

Carter looked down. "You did that."

The man put his finger on Carter's chest. "No, friend, *you* did that."

"Don't touch me."

The man shrugged and put his hands in his pockets. "If you hadn't hit that one agent, we would have never been able to arrest him." He chuckled. "Word is that Director Hoover is mighty steamed about that."

"What do you mean?"

The agent ignored his question and said, "Anyway, then there's that unfortunate accident that poor Mr. Bonnist had at 9th and Irving." He clicked his tongue and shook his head. "Real tragedy. A wife and three kids." The man stopped and put his hand on his chest. "But I guess people like you don't care about wives and kids."

Don't kill the G-man! Don't kill the G-man!

"Are you done?" asked Carter through gritted teeth.

"Well, then there's the best one of 'em all. Best one for last, you might say. An *international* incident." He sighed and looked across the street. "I feel sorry for the rube from the State Department who has to explain to the Czechoslovakian Foreign Ministry that sometimes walking in San Francisco can be hazardous to your health." He lowered his voice and hissed. "Particularly if you get on the wrong side of Nick Williams." The man cocked his. "Right?"

Carter turned and headed down Hyde, crossing Filbert without checking for traffic.

"We're watching you," said the man just loud enough to be heard.

. . .

Carter got out of the Yellow Cab in front of the old Mint. He walked over to the phone booth that was at the corner of Mission and in front of the Provident Loan building. He inserted a dime before dialing the phone number of Sam's place on Jessie.

As the line began to ring, he realized the *Chronicle* building was right across the street. He'd forgotten it was across Mission from the old Mint. In the map of the City that he carried around in his head, they weren't

193

that close to each other. That didn't make any sense, but it was true. After four rings, he heard Sam say, "Hello?"

"It's Carter."

"You think I did it, don't you?"

"I don't know what to think."

"I don't have access to a beat-up black Chevy, I try to stay out of the Sunset District if I can, and I wasn't anywhere near Chinatown last night. I was with Ike. We went to eat at the Compton's on Turk. Then we saw *The Last Time I Saw Paris* at the Warfield. After that we ducked into the Silver Rail."

"We were at the Silver Rail and we didn't see you."

"I know. We left through the tunnel below as soon as you and Nick stumbled in around midnight." Sam chuckled. "You two could barely stand upright. On the way back to North Beach, we had a big fight, which is why I'm here and not there. Satisfied?"

"Then who did it?"

"Hell, if I know. I thought it was you until I checked around."

"I beg your fuckin' pardon. You did what?"

"I was a real asshole to you, yesterday, and I was afraid maybe me runnin' off at the mouth the way I did made you lose your head or something."

"Seriously?" asked Carter, realizing he was partially furious and partially tickled that Sam thought he was capable of doing such a thing. It was a deeply uncomfortable feeling, to say the least.

"Yeah, seriously. But I checked up on you. You and Nick went to Ernie's. Then you went to the Black Cat." He laughed. "There are a number of queens who are hopping mad that you won't let them sit in your lap."

"So, I'm in the clear, then?" Carter was still angry, but it was fading.

"Yes, you are."

"Then who did it?"

"I dunno."

"Was it a coincidence?"

"Hell, no, it was most definitely not."

"Maybe Ferdinand?"

"Nope. I was at your place first thing this morning and grilled Anna about that."

"Oh... that's why Gustav went out and bought a copy of the *Examiner* this morning."

"Probably."

Neither man spoke for a moment.

"Carter?"

"Yes?"

"I want you to know I love you both and I know I've been giving you a rough time with all this."

"Well—"

"Hold on. In spite of what I said yesterday, you're turning out to be a better private dick than I would have thought possible."

Carter couldn't decide whether he should be offended or not.

"There's one loose end, though," added Sam.

"What?"

"The F.B.I."

"Not really. The one agent who talked to me yesterday—the one who told me I was messing up their operation—he cornered me about twenty minutes ago."

"Where?"

"Hyde and Filbert."

"What were you doing up there?"

Carter took a deep breath. "Taking care of business."

"This is that thing you wouldn't tell me about, right?"

"Right." Carter pressed his lips together. "It was Zelda."

"Zelda?"

"She worked for Dr. Williams from before Nick's mother left until we moved in."

"Oh, right. Anna took her job."

"Yes."

"What about her?"

"She's the one who told Bonnist about Mike falsifying records."

"How much did he pay her?"

Carter chuckled. "I have no idea. But..."

"What?"

"Nothing."

"Tell me, Carter," said Sam with a sing-song voice. "Come on," he teased. "Don't be shy."

That made Carter laugh. "Is that how you talk to Ike in bed?"

"Sometimes."

Carter laughed again. "I love you, too, Sam. Thanks for taking care of Nick."

"I'm taking care of you, too, Red."

"Don't call me that and I know. Thanks."

"So...?"

"Oh! So, what I was going to say was that I thought Zelda was relieved when I confronted her about Bonnist. I think she was expecting me to confront her about something else."

"Interesting. Any idea what?"

"No." Carter chuckled to himself. "But it is kinda creepy in her apartment."

"Yeah?"

"She can see our house from her living room."

"That *is* creepy."

"Definitely."

"Where are you, by the way?" asked Sam.

"I'm around the corner from your place in the phone

booth next to the pawn shop and across from the old Mint. I wanted to call before knocking on your door."

Sam laughed. "Lemme take you to breakfast or get you a cup of coffee."

"I'd like that, Sam, I really would. But I have one more thing I need to do before I meet Nick at the marina."

"Goin' out sailin' with Cap'n O'Reilly, be you?" asked Sam in an Irish brogue.

"Yes."

Neither man spoke for a moment.

"Sam?"

"Yeah?"

"Thanks."

"You're welcome, Red," replied Sam before the line went dead.

. . .

Carter dropped another dime into the phone and dialed Mike's home phone number. After three rings, Greg Holland, his lover, answered. "Hello?"

"Hi, Greg. It's Carter."

"Hi! How are you? Are we still going out on the bay at noon? Please tell me we are!"

Carter laughed. "As far as I know, we are. Is Mike there?"

"He's at the office. He's going from there to meet us at the marina. Do you need anything?"

"I'll just call him there. See you at noon."

"Definitely!"

. . .

Carter was in another Yellow Cab and headed for the office when he remembered that he was still checked in at the Hotel Californian.

Once the driver dropped him off in front, he walked into the lobby and over to the counter where, to his surprise, the same guy from before was working. The man seemed to be waiting for him. And he was frowning.

"Well, good mornin'! And how are you?" exclaimed Carter as Howard T. Albertson. "Don't they ever let you go home?"

"Yes, they do." The man paused. "Mr. Jones."

Carter took a deep breath. In his normal voice, he said, "I'm here to check out."

"That seems like a good idea."

"I'll just go upstairs and—"

"No need, sir. Your belongings are with the bellman."

Carter nodded and started to turn.

"Would you like your receipt and the balance due you from the hotel, Mr. Jones?"

He smiled at the man, as he thought about what Nick would do. It was probably somewhere around 80 bucks. "No. Keep it and donate it or throw a party for the staff with it."

The man nodded. "Very well. Have a nice day, Mr. Jones."

. . .

Carter got out of the Veteran's Cab in front of the office and pulled his two valises out with him. He opened the door, walked into what could be loosely described as a lobby and then walked up the two flights to the third floor.

After stopping at his office to drop off his luggage and hide it under his desk, he made his way down the hall and knocked on Mike's half-opened door. "Hello?"

"Carter?"

"Have a sec?" asked Carter as he walked in. Mike was leaning back in his chair and smoking a cigar with his feet up on his desk. He was obviously dressed for going out on the yacht since he was wearing khaki trousers with crepe-soled shoes.

Looking over with a smile, he asked, "Is this about going out on the bay?"

Carter sat in the chair next to Mike's desk with a laugh. "I just talked to Greg and he asked the same thing."

"We were working on the house this morning when Nick called." Mike took a big puff of his cigar. "I don't think either of us wants to strip anymore wallpaper. Maybe not for a while. Going out on the bay is the excuse we both need."

"Happy to oblige."

Mike sat up and put his feet on the floor. "What brings you by?"

Carter took a deep breath. "There's something I need to tell you about that I don't wany anyone else to know."

Mike began to frown in that way that could easily scare anyone who didn't know him. Nick called it his "monster face." He asked, "What's wrong?"

It's lying time again.

"Someone leaked the truth about what happened the day Dr. Williams shot Marty Cox."

Mike's eyebrows shot up. "Are you serious?"

Carter nodded. "I don't know how it happened, but I was told about it." He shifted a little. "I know what you wrote on your report."

"Who told you?"

"No one connected to the police. In fact, I'm not sure

199

how my source knew."

"*Your* source? Since when do you have sources?"

Maybe this was not a good idea.

"Bad choice of words," conceded Carter.

Mike bit down on his cigar and closed his eyes for a moment. He said, "Damn," as he exhaled a puff of smoke that went right into Carter's face.

"I wouldn't worry about it. I just wanted you to know that it did get out."

Mike opened his eyes and glared at Carter. "This is not the time to be fuckin' around with me. I need to know how you know and who told you."

"I'll tell you, but I don't want Nick to know."

"Why not?"

Time to come clean. A little... maybe...

Carter leaned back. He ran his hand over his mouth. "Nick already knows, actually."

Mike took his cigar out of his mouth and stared at Carter for a long moment. "This must be some serious bad news for you to be lying like you are. You never lie."

If you only knew...

"It's one of your annoying character flaws."

"Character flaw?"

"Skip it. Tell me everything."

Carter opened his mouth to speak...

This is my company, asshole.

He closed his mouth and then said, "No."

"No?"

Carter stood. "I came here to tell you the one thing that you need to know and that's the fact that, somehow, at least one person in town, besides me and Nick, know that you falsified the report on how Marty Cox died."

After dropping his cigar into an ashtray, Mike got to his feet. Since he was wearing crepe-soled shoes and

Carter was wearing his usual leather shoes, they were both looking at each other right in the eye. Normally, Carter had to look up just a bit since Mike had an inch on him. "Look, you son-of-a-bitch," said Mike, "this is my ass that's on the line here. I need to know everything." He poked Carter in the chest. "*Everything.*"

In a calm and even voice, Carter said, "Do that again and you'll be in traction."

"So, that's how it is, huh?"

"That's how it is in this case, yes."

With a deepening frown, Mike asked "*Case?*"

"In this instance."

Mike moved towards him just about an inch. "What are you up to, Carter?"

"When I want you to know, I'll tell you."

His electric blue eyes searched Carter's. After a long and very tense moment, he stepped back. "Fine. But it's your ass I'll be kickin' if somethin' comes down on my head and I don't know it's comin' because you've been withholding information."

"You're not a cop anymore."

Mike nodded as he picked up his cigar and looked at it. "You're right about that." He then gave Carter a tight grin and whispered, "I can get away with shit now that I couldn't then."

"And you work for me."

"I work for Nick."

"Same difference."

Mike put his cigar in his mouth and said, "Speaking of work, I've got some of my own to do before we set sail. So, if you'll excuse me..."

I can't leave it this way. I owe him my gratitude, if nothing else.

"Mike?"

The other man plopped down, put his feet back up on

his desk, and grabbed a folder from a pile to his right. "What?"

"Thank you. For everything."

Mike sighed. He put the cigar back in its ashtray and the folder back on its pile. He then put his feet on the floor and stood. Turning to Carter, he said, "You're welcome."

Carter lifted his hand to pat Mike on the shoulder, but Mike grabbed him before he could do so and pulled him in for an unexpected hug. Mike whispered in his ear, "I love you, Carter. I don't know why, but I do. That said... One of these days..."

"I know, Mike. Neither of us can fuck the other, so we're gonna end up in a knock-out, drag-out fight one of these days. Just like the cowboys do in the movies."

Mike burst out laughing, kissed Carter on his ear, and squeezed him tight.

Author's Note

If this was your first Nick & Carter book, you might want to try the very first novel I wrote: *The Unexpected Heiress*, the first title in the Nick Williams Mysteries series. It's all about the death of Nick's sister, Janet, and the unexpected things that happen in Nick's and Carter's lives as a result.

You could also explore how Nick and Carter met in *An Enchanted Beginning*.

Or... you could read the next book that, chronologically, follows this one in the world of Nick and Carter: *The Timid Traitor*. It begins in January of 1955, about six weeks after this story ends.

. . .

This story, like all the others I've written, came to me out of thin air.

Many thanks, as always, to everyone who has read, reviewed, and emailed me about all of my books. It is deeply gratifying in ways that words will never be able to fully express. Thank you.

. . .

For news about upcoming books, subscribe to my newsletter here:

https://frankwbutterfield.com/subscribe

Acknowledgments

I relied on *Army Fire Fighting: A Historical Perspective* by Leroy Allen Ward for the details in the prologue covering Brian Radcliff's firefighting service in the Army and his assignment to Pusan during the Korean War.

All of my references to current events came from the archived pages of the *San Francisco Examiner* and the *San Mateo Times* on Newspapers.com and *The New York Times* on TimesMachine. References to businesses and addresses came via the *Examiner* and the *San Mateo Times* as well as *Polk's San Francisco City Directory 1953* made available on archive.org through the San Francisco Public Library. I referred to a 1953 Standard Oil street map for street directions courtesy of the David Rumsey Map Collection.

Special thanks to Ron Perry for his help with the cover template for this new series.

As always, many thanks to my mother for her gift of telling a good story. Love you!

Thanks, once again, to Edward Lane and Acacia Tally for their patronage of this book!

Historical Notes

The events in this story take place between Tuesday, November 23, 1954 and Saturday, November 27, 1954.

First off, I must admit that, like Carter, I too have lied in the telling of this tale. During that Thanksgiving weekend, the Bay Area was socked in pretty bad with not only fog but what was likely some of the worst smog to hit the place. I was almost finished, however, when I realized this. So, I ask your forgiveness for making all those late November days of 1954 to be summer-like for our hero. A thousand apologies for misleading you, dear reader.

In our story, we visit the Hotel Californian at the corner of Taylor and O'Farrell. In 1954, this facility was owned by the Glide Foundation (connected to Glide Memorial Methodist Church two blocks away which, after the Reverend Cecil Williams became its pastor in 1963, as some readers will know, become a significant force in the early gay rights movement as well as during the AIDS crisis and beyond). It was advertised as a temperance hotel.

Those familiar with the San Francisco cable car lines may be wondering why Nick and Carter took a cab to Aquatic Park instead of walking down Sacramento to Hyde Street to take the cable car line that runs from Hyde to Beach and would have put them right where Nick's hot dog vendor had his cart. The old O'Farrell-Hyde-Jones line (whose northern terminus was at Hyde and Bay) was discontinued in April of 1954. The new Powell-Hyde line (which today ends at Hyde and Beach just outside the Buena Vista Café) didn't start running until 1957. So, there was, sadly, no cable car for them to take in November of 1954.

Everyone who appears in this story is fictional. The person referenced in the title of this book, a man we never see, and Ferdinand's stalker from afar was a real person, however.

Antonín Novotný was born in 1904 in Letňany (now a suburb of Prague) when it was under the rule of the Austro-Hungarian Empire. He was a charter member of the Communist Party of Czechoslovakia (CPC) when it was founded in 1921. During the German occupation, he was an active member of the underground until he was arrested in 1941. He was sent to the Mauthausen concentration camp in what is now Austria and was liberated by American forces in 1945. After the war, he worked his way through the upper echelons of the CPC leadership and was elected First Secretary in the fall of 1953. In 1957, he also became President of Czechoslovakia. He retained both positions until he was removed from both offices and resigned from the party during the events of the Prague Spring in 1968. In 1971, he was rehabilitated by the CPC and passed away in 1975.

Novotný was not well-educated. He'd trained as a locksmith and was likely given the usual political instruction by the party apparatus. His real skill was his ability to network within the party and inside the Soviet sphere. He was not charismatic, but he knew who to talk to (or cajole, lean on, or blackmail) in order to get things done. It's likely he sabotaged his First Secretary predecessor who was removed after being accused of Titoism. That removal paved the way for Novotný to take the position and become the most powerful man in the country.

It's very unlikely that a man with his position in the party would have attended the 1952 Olympics, but it's a good way to explain who he is in relationship to Ferdinand.

Novotný was married and had one son. During his lifetime, he was referred to as "schöne Tony," a German phrase that means "beautiful Tony." It was also rumored that, during a United Nations visit, he was elected the most handsome statesman from among all the delegates. Both of these anecdotes were intended to be disparaging by those who recounted them.

Was Novotný gay or bisexual? I found no direct evidence that this was the case other than the fact that, in my opinion, he had what an old roommate of mine called "the gay eyes" (insert LOL here). Along with the disparaging remarks about his attractiveness (which, in my opinion, has historically been a discreet way of accusing a man of being gay), the one thing that jumps out at me is that there are several references online about how he was notably devoted to attending the Spartakiáda which were mass public gymnastic events held regularly in Czechoslovakia. That's not evidence, in and of itself, but it did raise a flag in my mind and is enough for me to use Novotný's position and power as a motivating force in this story.

Credits

Yesteryear Font (headings) used with permission under SIL Open Font License, Version 1.1. Copyright © 2011 by Brian J. Bonislawsky DBA Astigmatic (AOETI). All rights reserved.

Gentium Book Basic Font (body text) used with permission under the SIL Open Font License, Version 1.1. Copyright © 2002 by J. Victor Gaultney. All rights reserved.

Oswald Font (cover) used with permission under the SIL Open Font License, Version 1.1. Copyright © 2016 by The Oswald Project Authors. All rights reserved.

Gladifilthefte Font (cover) by Tup Wanders used under a Creative Commons license by attribution.

My Underwood Font (telegrams) used with permission. Copyright © 2009 by Tension Type. All rights reserved.

Cover design consulting by Ron Perry Graphic Design. Find out more about Ron and the wonderful work he does here: rperrydesign.com

More Information

Be the first to know about new releases:

frankwbutterfield.com